Funf Mann

A Prisoner of War Story

James H. Burke - 1943

Funf Mann

A Prisoner of War Story

by

James H. Burke

MEREDITH PRESS
SKANEATELES, NEW YORK

Meredith Press
54 East Elizabeth Street
Skaneateles, New York 13152

Front and Back Cover Sketch by Lisa Emmi
Illustrations by John Mahaffy

ISBN 0-9640884-0-1

*This is a work of fiction, based on the
author's actual experience. No criticism of
any person, living or dead, is intended.*

This book is dedicated to my wife June, who shared the post-war effects of this experience with me.

1994 Photo of the Author

Mr. Burke graduated from Oswego High School in 1942. He entered military service in March 1943. The 299th Engineer Combat Battalion was part of the initial assault forces landing in Normandy on D-Day. During the Bulge they maintained a defensive line of bridges which they blew up as the German tanks advanced. Mr. Burke spent five months as a Prisoner of War in Germany, which is the basis for the story in his book. After the war Mr. Burke married June Marie Cady. He attended Syracuse University, during which period their first two children were born. A third child was born shortly after he graduated in 1950 with a degree in Mechanical Engineering. After thirty-five years as Sales Engineer for Power Transmission Equipment, he retired in 1985 to Skaneateles, New York, the home town of his wife.

It is not the critic who counts—not the man who points out how the strong man stumbled, or where the doer of deed could have done better. The credit belongs to the man who is actually in the arena; whose face is marred by dust and sweat and blood; who strives valiantly; who errs, and who comes short again and again. It is he who knows the great enthusiasm, the great devotions, and spends himself in a worthy cause; who at best knows in the end the triumphs of high achievement; and who, at the worst, if he fails, at least fails while daring greatly so that his place shall never be with those cold and timid souls who know neither defeat nor victory.

—Theodore Roosevelt

Table of Contents

Illustrations

Introduction

On December 16, 1944, the German Army launched an offensive that has since been well documented as the Battle of the Bulge. Like all other battles in war, the real heroes are those that died in the course of battle. Relatives of the deceased and the seriously wounded endured the most suffering in this battle. Among the survivors were those that became Prisoners of War. This book is the story of one such Prisoner of War during his five months of captivity.

Chapter I

APPELL

"Funf mann, funf mann," the German sergeant shouted as he moved from left to right down the line, at the same time moving his left arm up and down in a vertical sweep to indicate he wanted the prisoners to line up in rows of five, front to back. Corporal Jimmy Burns, the fifth man in the second row, stood there thinking about how many times he had heard that command and how annoyed he became each time they had been lined up in this manner for a head count.

Here he was, twenty years old, a prisoner of war, standing in line at Stalag 2D near Stargard, Germany. He did not know exactly where the POW camp was located, although he had been told that it was close to the Baltic Sea. The prisoners had determined the location by reading road signs as they marched into the camp a few weeks ago. The only two things he was sure of were that it was bitter cold, and that it was the middle of March 1945. He had been a prisoner of war for three months, having been captured by the Germans in December 1944, during the *Battle of the Bulge.* Although the Allied Forces had since regained all territory lost in this battle, Jimmy Burns was still a prisoner of the Germans.

Stalag 2D resembled a military base, except that barbed wire surrounded the entire perimeter of the camp. The fences were ten feet high. A second fence, equally as high, extended beyond the inner fence, and rolls of barbed wire looped, accordion fashion, between the two fences. A final barrier to escape was a three-strand band of barbed wire that angled inward, on top of each fence, to prevent climbing straight up and over. A single strand of wire, three feet high, was located twelve feet inside the inner fence to keep prisoners from touching this fence. Signs hung on the single strand warning in German that the main fences were electrically charged. On each corner and at selected intervals guard towers were in place, complete with machine guns and searchlights.

All buildings in the camp were a drab gray color; they were made of unpainted, weathered boards. Open areas between the buildings were very muddy, due to an earlier thaw that had turned snow into a cold rain. The prisoners ran from building to building, turning the area in between into a quagmire.

The total distance around the perimeter of the camp was probably two to three miles. Separate compounds within the camp were partitioned off by wire fences with gates that opened for passage in and out of the various compounds.

The other compounds at Stalag 2D contained French, Russian, and various Slavic groups, all confined to separate areas. Each day the Americans would see work parties leaving the other compounds, but because the Americans were all non-commissioned officers they were exempted from work details. Evidently, Stalag 2D had been erected next to a military hospital (called *lazerett* in German) to provide a labor force with which to maintain the hospital facilities.

The Americans were housed in a compound previously occupied by civilian political prisoners. These prisoners were usually Jewish and could be identified by the black and white striped uniforms they wore. Every day they marched down the road, in full view of the Americans, heading for work at the hospital.

When the Americans arrived at Stalag 2D they were all exhausted and very sick, having just completed a fifteen day railroad trip in boxcars. The Americans soon realized that there were many other prisoners in worse shape than themselves, especially the Jewish civilians in the striped suits.

Jimmy Burns had grown up in a small community in upstate New York. Life was dull for a teenager during the latter years of the *Great Depression*. World War II came along at just the right time to provide excitement for boys the age of Jimmy Burns. Many of his friends had left high school to enlist in military service, but the parents of Jimmy Burns insisted he stay in school until graduation. Being second generation Irish-Catholic, his parents believed that education and hard work were the American way to improve one's status in life.

Shortly after Jimmy's eighteenth birthday, the Selective Service System—or draft, as it was commonly called—sent him the usual *Greetings*, and assigned him to the U.S. Army.

Since early childhood, Jimmy Burns had always thought a military career was surely the way he wanted to spend his life; after two years of duty in World War II, he was beginning to have some doubts. *Now*, as he stood in line being counted, he was absolutely certain it was not going to work out for him. Even if he lived through this POW ordeal, most likely the Army would discharge him as a coward for having been captured.

Growing up in a town that had a military post within its city limits had helped point Jimmy Burns in the direction of an Army career. He spent many days watching recruits drill and soldiers performing daily duties; heard bugle calls and observed parades and formations. Before he was ten years old, Jimmy Burns knew the difference between infantry, artillery, and calvary. He knew the Army command arrangement, from Squad all the way up to Division. Jimmy had seen airplanes fly into the military fort and snatch messages from a wire line stretched between posts on the ground. At the time this was considered to be an advanced method of relaying information between units.

Jimmy Burns admired soldiers for their dedication to duty. They constantly practiced for war that might never come.

Anyway, here he was—sick, cold, feeling miserable and disappointed—standing beside his buddy, Corporal Jim Kelsey, being counted for the umpteenth time. The snow on the ground made a *crunchy* sound as he stomped his feet in an effort to keep them warm. The German sergeant continued to bellow, "*Funf mann, funf mann,*" trying to make himself heard over the noise of hundreds of stomping feet.

The Germans called it *appell*, which in English meant roll call. The Germans did not call out names: they simply lined everyone up in rows of five, and then counted left to right, "*Eins, zwei, drei,*" etc., until the last row was reached. Simple arithmetic of multiplying the number of rows by five gave them the total number of prisoners standing in the formation. This procedure was repeated at least once every day, obviously to make certain no one had escaped overnight or during the day, when a work party or other special detail left the camp briefly.

The complete counting process easily could have been completed in ten to fifteen minutes. It frequently took an hour or more when the prisoners, or *kriegies* as they called themselves, chose not to cooperate. *Kriegie* was a shortened version of the German word *kriegsgefangene*—which most of the prisoners could neither pronounce nor remember—meaning prisoner of war.

The Germans were fastidious about this counting business. If anyone moved during the count, or a blank spot existed, or even if the rows were not straight, the sergeant stopped the count and started all over again, "*Eins, zwei,*

4

drei," etc. He usually stopped the count with an outburst like, "*Ach du lieber,*" "*Funf mann, funf mann,*" "The *kommandant* will not dismiss you until the count is completed," or, "The guards have been ordered to shoot the next man to leave the formation."

At this point about fifteen or twenty *kriegies* would break ranks and head for the latrine. Almost all the men had dysentery. Fifteen minutes was about as long as anyone could hold it without crapping in his pants. A guard would fire a warning shot or two, either into the air or into the ground; this didn't deter those in dire need of the facilities. Even the guard stationed at the entrance to the latrine was sympathetic to this urgency and would only stop prisoners briefly to try to determine if they were faking it.

Jimmy Burns knew that this particular morning the *appell* was going to be slow, because on the way out the door a member of the American commander's staff had told the prisoners to delay the count in order that an escape in progress could gain some time. The Germans must have been tipped off, because this morning the roll call began much earlier than usual.

"What the hell was going on?" Jimmy Burns wondered.

He also wondered how a German guard would feel about shooting a prisoner of war just because the poor bastard wanted to get out of this filthy place.

Although escape attempts were common and actually encouraged, success was practically nil. Almost always, within a few days, the *kriegies* usually showed up again in the same camp. They probably had not gone very far before being recaptured.

Jimmy Burns was surprised to hear that an escape was *on* that morning, because he and his buddy Jim Kelsey had been turned down by the escape committee just a few days ago when they had presented their own plan for an escape.

The American prisoners were governed by a camp commander, traditionally the ranking sergeant in the camp.

He had a staff that bunked with him in a separate room in one of the barracks. His staff was comprised of one committee each for food, health, escape, communications, complaints, etc. The camp commander also had a staff member in each of the other barracks to help coordinate all activities of the various committees. The commander and his staff were supposed to look out for the welfare of the prisoners in the American compound. In this capacity he had the only direct contact with the German *kommandant* and his staff. Complaints centered around food, clothing, and sanitary conditions, all of which affected health and the general well-being of the prisoners. There were many complaints about treatment and conditions; these, however, were accorded little, if any, attention. Conditions seemed to get worse, the longer the men were confined.

The escape committee, if they approved an escape plan, would furnish escapees with food and extra clothing, as well as maps and instructions on when, where, who to look for, etc. They would also delay the count, as was being done this morning, but not unless they approved every detail of the escape in advance.

The communications committee had possession of a shortwave radio and listened every evening to news broadcasts from England. This committee prepared bulletins relating to the progress of the war, which they read to the prisoners each morning.

All activities of the escape and communications committees were, supposedly, kept secret from the Germans. There were, however, informers among the prisoners, and the Germans always had up-to-date information about these activities. Likewise, the American commander's staff had access to German secrets by bribing some of the guards with American cigarettes and other goodies that came in Red Cross parcels.

Neither Jimmy nor his buddy Kelsey had much contact with the staff because they were only corporals; the staff members were mainly high-ranking sergeants or pals of the commander (most probably from his old outfit). Even in a POW camp, the Army *caste* system prevailed.

Jimmy Burns and Jim Kelsey had become close friends during the past three months. Like Burns, Kelsey was also Irish-Catholic. They both had been raised in large families and could easily relate to each other's childhood experiences. The two were almost the same size, with Kelsey being slightly taller and thinner. Although they each had facial features that were typically Irish, neither of them came close to fitting the usual description of "a big Irishman." The main difference between the two was that Kelsey had lived in a large city, and therefore, had acquired *street smarts*. Kelsey's aggressiveness sometimes embarrassed Jimmy Burns, but Kelsey was able to look out for their best interests whenever an unfair situation arose. If a more diplomatic approach to a problem seemed in order, Jimmy Burns was given the assignment.

Kelsey's toughness reminded Jimmy Burns of his Uncle "Tip," the way they were both able to speak up to anyone, regardless of rank. Uncle Tip Barry was a career soldier in the United States Army. He held the highest rank attainable for an enlisted man: master sergeant. He had always been Jimmy Burns' favorite hero; the main reason that Jimmy had wanted to pursue an Army career.

How would Tip react if he were able to look in on this scene, right now? What would he think of Jimmy Burns for having become a prisoner of war?

Probably he'd say, "A good soldier does not surrender, he escapes, killing all the enemy in his path."

All regular Army soldiers talk tough when they are training recruits. They all talk about wanting to get where the fighting is, knowing they will be kept at home to train more recruits. Jimmy Burns knew only one other regular Army soldier; one that he also admired very much.

Eddie Boyd bunked with Jimmy Burns during basic

training. He became a sergeant after only a few weeks and had been a great influence on Jimmy Burns, further encouraging him to make the Army a career. Eddie Boyd had twelve years of regular Army under his belt when he showed up as a draftee, along with the eighteen-year-old boys who made up over ninety percent of the battalion. Eddie had dropped out of the service during the late thirties to return home and better support his family. Hell, he had a wife and five kids at home. He felt guilty about being left out of the fight, so he volunteered to be drafted at age forty-four.

Eddie was a tough little guy, but also very gentle when it came to handling men. He was shipped out as a cadreman right after basic training ended. His last words to Jimmy Burns had been, "Your uncle is probably a great guy, but remember, always remain a gentleman. It will come in handy later when you become an officer."

That's what Jimmy would tell Uncle Tip, "Hell, I'm tough too, but also a gentleman. I'm going to be an officer someday."

Jimmy Burns continued to stomp his feet trying to get them warm. The count on this day had started, stopped, and restarted several times. Kelsey suddenly squatted down on his haunches as if he were going to take a crap right there in the formation. Jimmy Burns knew that Kelsey was hiding from the German sergeant's view so the new count which was about to begin would be screwed up. As soon as the German sergeant saw the empty space he muttered an obscenity, then stomped down to the end of the line seeking a replacement. Kelsey stood up just as the replacement arrived. This was timed perfectly to coincide with the start of the new count so that the German sergeant would have to begin all over again. The sergeant admonished the replacement for wandering around the formation, having forgotten already that he had just sent him there to fill in a blank space. Antics like this were repeated over and over again. It was very difficult for the Germans to get an accurate count.

They stood in line an hour this morning. Both Jimmy Burns and Jim Kelsey had been to the latrine twice. They had talked about many things, including the possibility that the story about an escape being in progress was probably "pure bullshit." How in the hell could there be an escape going on when they had been told that escapes were forbidden at this time? Of course, anyone could try an escape on his own, but he wouldn't get very far without the escape committee's help. Burns and Kelsey decided the commander had another reason to delay the count this morning. Of course, he was not about to share his plans with the rest of them

As the count continued, Jimmy Burns suddenly became oblivious to all the commotion around him, and his thoughts slowly drifted back in time to the beginning of this odyssey. Jimmy could still hear the German sergeant shouting *funf mann*, but the voice seemed to be coming from the past.

When Jimmy Burns first heard this strange expression, *funf mann*, he was with a group of fewer than thirty men, having just been captured in a small Belgian town called Martelange. His mind continued to drift backward to the start of the whole thing: the invasion of Normandy on D-Day. Jimmy Burns found himself recalling almost every day, right up to this very moment, while he stood there in line, stomping his feet to try to keep them warm. Some of the best days of his Army life had been spent in Hovelange, Luxembourg; and the worst, of course, had been all those days that followed, after capture in Martelange, Belgium.

Among these thoughts, his Uncle Tip's voice kept repeating, "What kind of a soldier winds up in a prisoner of war camp?"

Sergeant Eddie Boyd was also advising him, "Keep cool, tough it out. A soldier's life takes a lot of crazy turns. You can make it."

Funny, he thought, how he kept remembering Uncle Tip and Eddie Boyd at the same time. One was reminding him that he was a failure. The other was more tolerant of the situation. Which hero should he listen to?

Chapter II

INVASION

Of all the combat engineer battalions assigned to the European Theater, the 299th was unique, due to the common bond that existed among its enlisted men (nonofficers). They were all draftees who had lived within one hundred miles of each other in upstate New York. Like Jimmy Burns, many were recent high school graduates, and most knew at least a dozen men from their own home town. A *camaraderie* had developed in the 299th, right from the start of training, which resulted in the battalion becoming a powerful force in combat.

A combat engineer battalion is made up of about six hundred men, with the total being divided equally among four companies of one hundred fifty men each. All engineer battalions receive training in a variety of construction duties, but roads and bridges are the primary concern. Because combat engineer battalions perform their duties at or near the front, they also receive training in infantry tactics. Furthermore, combat engineers are often called upon to split into groups as small as fourteen (squad size), but most of the jobs require a full platoon (forty-five men).

The first combat experience for the 299th came on D-Day during the invasion of Normandy. Kelsey and Burns were members of B Company, which drew Utah Beach as its assignment. For some unknown reason the operation at

11

Omaha Beach required only two companies of the battalion to participate in the assault. The battalion commander said he couldn't choose between the three line companies, so he had the company commanders flip a coin to determine which company would be left behind. Company B lost the coin toss, which at the time seemed that they were getting *screwed* again.

Company B was assigned to a Naval underwater demolition task force for the assault on Utah Beach. They left the battalion and went to train with the Navy aboard a landing ship tank (LST), far down the coast of England. Aboard ship things were pretty good; seasickness made food unimportant. On land, the Navy doesn't feed its troops as well, so the boys of Company B griped constantly about the raw deal they were getting.

They stayed in Nissen huts, which look like Quonset huts, but are made of cement. At this point no one could foresee what a stroke of good fortune this assignment would become.

When the invasion finally came, the men were so sick of practice landings the actual landing relieved all the frustration and tension that had been building. History books all record Utah Beach as something of a *cakewalk*. Anyone that was there with B Company of the 299th would dispute this claim. The story line always states that the assault troops of the Fourth Infantry Division met little opposition because they landed a mile off course due to winds and tide. The fact is they landed off course due to elimination of three of the four navigational vessels that were supposed to be anchored to outline the boundaries of the invasion area. One vessel dropped out because its anchor line fouled the propeller shaft. Another struck a mine, and a third was sunk by German coastal batteries. The fourth navigational vessel wound up eventually right where it belonged: on the Western boundary of the invasion area. Although the combined Navy-engineer demolition teams were supposed to be in the fourth and fifth waves, they all landed without the benefit of assault troops in front of them. The landing point was opposite Exit Four, a heavily fortified section of Utah Beach.

The small landing craft containing Jimmy Burns and his group bobbed up and down as it turned in circles some distance from the big LST. They were forming up with the other landing craft in a line, or wave, as the Navy called it.

Aboard the number one boat was a Navy commander named Petersen, who was in charge of the demolition task force at Utah Beach. When the other seven boats were in a line, Commander Petersen gave a heading to his coxswain and advised the signalman to relay the information to the rest of the wave. There were no radios aboard these little boats. Complete radio silence was in effect anyway; had been ever since the entire invasion fleet put to sea two days ago. Seasickness among the Army men was not a problem now. They had heaved every morsel of food that had been consumed in the last two days. The big high-protein breakfast of steak and eggs served that morning had gone pretty well untouched by the soldiers.

Jimmy Burns was crouched against the rear bulkhead of the landing craft. From this position he could hear conversation between Commander Petersen and the Navy crew. After several short conversations regarding heading and directions to the signalman for relay to the other boats, the coxswain said, "Sir, the other waves on our portside are veering off to the southeast. Do you want me to follow them?"

The commander looked at the compass, then at the navigational vessel that was bobbing up and down off his starboard bow and said, "No, keep the heading you're on. We're going to land where we are supposed to."

A few more signals were relayed with the signal lamp, and the coxswain repeated, "Sir, the rest of the invasion force is now out of sight. Do you want me to change course?"

"No," the commander replied. "Keep this heading."

Jimmy Burns stood straight up to see what was ahead. In the hazy mist, he saw what looked like land and the tremendous flash of a large gun firing out to sea. A sick feeling crept into his stomach, and his legs became weak, causing him to slide back down on his haunches. He had hardly crouched down again when the landing craft came to an abrupt halt. The ramp was opened and everyone piled out of the little boat into waist deep water.

One of the squad members, nicknamed Monk, said to his friend Kozar, "Jesus, Nick, somebody's shooting at us."

The shooting came as a surprise to most of the men, even though they had been warned to expect it. All the practice runs had been performed without anyone shooting at them. It was assumed all along that infantry assault troops would have the beach well under control when the demolition squads arrived. There was always the chance that opposition would be stronger than expected, but this had been discounted as only a remote possibility. When practicing in England, the only explosions the men had seen or heard were the small charges they had set off to simulate blowing the beach obstacles. They usually applied dummy packs, went through the motions of blowing the obstacles, removed the packs, and repeated the process over and over again.

There was one exception to this routine of practice without the existence of enemy interruption. One night while waiting to disembark for a practice landing, the men of the 299th saw ships well to their rear on fire and heard the repeated noise of explosions. The practice went on as usual at dawn, but everyone seemed panicky that morning and rumors abounded. No information was released about this incident until long after the war was over. When the facts were finally reported, they revealed that German torpedo boats had slipped in amongst the convoy of LSTs, sunk one, and damaged three others. Approximately seven hundred fifty American soldiers and sailors lost their lives that night, more than a month before the real invasion took place.

As Jimmy Burns left the landing craft on the actual D-Day, the first thing he noticed was a German machine gun firing from behind the seawall. There was also a small bunker to his left from which a larger gun was firing. The first men out of the boats were racing to the seawall and to the rear of the bunker. Many men had fallen wounded and lay writhing in pain at the water's edge. The Germans along the seawall and in the bunker were overcome quickly by the superior number of attacking demolition teams. It took another half hour to round up the rest of the Germans further down the beach and herd them into a depression in the sand dunes, where they were held captive.

To his right, Jimmy Burns heard the roar of a large gun and could see the flash of its fire coming from a pillbox way up the beach. There were no troops to his right, only a long stretch of sandy beach without obstacles. This gun continued to fire at the engineers and Navy frogmen as they went about their duties of blowing beach obstacles. Artillery shells from enemy guns located further inland were landing on the beach area as the demolition work continued. Several of Jimmy Burns' friends were wounded that morning.

Finally, follow-up infantry troops of the Fourth Division landed, along with a few tanks, and the situation became more manageable.

Both Uncle Tip and Eddie Boyd would have been proud of Jimmy Burns for his behavior that day on Utah Beach. He performed his duty as if it were another practice run, without realizing any fear or panic. Jimmy's job was to place his demolition pack on the farthest obstacle out from shore, then string primer cord and connect it to other packs that had been placed on the row of obstacles. At the shoreline he assembled and ignited a manual fuze. The detonator wires had already been attached and strung out to the seawall, where his squad sergeant was waiting to activate it if the manual fuze failed to ignite the charges. As Jimmy Burns started to run to the seawall, a tremendous explosion lifted him off his feet, hurling him to within a yard or two of the seawall. Either the manual fuze ignited prematurely, or the sergeant activated the detonator too soon. Jimmy Burns was stunned, having traveled about fifty yards in the air before landing on his belly in soft sand.

As Jimmy Burns rolled over onto his back, he looked straight up into the face of his platoon leader, Lieutenant Russell.

"Are you OK?" Lieutenant Russell asked.

"I think so," Jimmy Burns replied.

"Good," said the lieutenant. "Now find some men with demolition packs, and get them up here to the seawall so we can blow a breach in it."

A rubber raft with backup demolitions was sitting at the water line, from which several men were helping themselves to the contents.

Jimmy Burns took six men and their packs up to the seawall where they placed them at the base of the wall. After installing and igniting a fuze, the group moved back to the water line, out of range of the explosion. The *blow* was a good one, opening up an eight foot gap in the wall.

Jimmy Burns was crouched beside a tank that was firing at the big pillbox far up the beach. It wasn't doing much damage from that distance, even though it was scoring hit after hit on the pillbox. The pillbox was firing at the tank, but overshooting its target by a considerable margin.

Jimmy banged his rifle against the tank, trying to get the attention of those inside. The tankers must not have heard him because there was no reply from inside the tank. Finally, the hatch opened and empty shell casings came flying out of the tank. Jimmy Burns was then able to get the attention of the tank commander and pointed out the hole in the seawall to him.

The tank moved quickly to the opening, climbed over the rubble, and started down the dune line toward the pillbox. A squad of infantry followed the tank. Shortly afterward, the big pillbox was knocked out, allowing the demolition teams to finish their work without worrying about the gun.

After a couple of hours, all obstacles in that sector of the beach were blown, so the demolition teams moved inland with the infantry.

All told, the number of men killed at Utah Beach that day was considered small, but Jimmy Burns saw a number of his friends being evacuated as wounded, along with a sizeable number of German prisoners that were captured by the demolition teams. German artillery from far inland continued to pound the beach throughout the day and well into the night.

Over at Omaha Beach, the story is well documented. Everything that could go wrong, went wrong. Both A and C Companies of the 299th suffered heavy casualties. At each beach the plan was the same. Individual soldiers landed with packs of demolitions strapped to their backs which they placed on the obstacles, strung out primer cord, and blew a single row of obstacles after everyone had cleared the area.

Each group was followed in by a rubber raft loaded with more demolition packs with which to repeat the process, until a sufficiently wide gap had been made in the field of obstacles. This was done to clear shipping lanes for larger boats to reach the shoreline with more troops and supplies.

Finally, all obstacles would be cleared. The engineers became infantrymen, and proceeded inland for further assignment.

One particular·piece of bad luck occurred at Omaha when a German shell hit one of the rubber rafts, exploding the entire load including the men that navigated the raft to shore. This incident sent six very good friends of Jimmy

17

Burns to a watery grave. Most of their remains were never recovered. Jimmy Burns learned from Kelsey one day that he, too, had lost friends from his home town on Omaha Beach.

Companies A and C performed their duties under most difficult conditions, and casualties ran very high that day. Later, a Presidential Unit Citation was awarded the battalion for its efforts on Omaha Beach.

As nighttime fell on Utah Beach (rather late due to military observance of double daylight saving time), the second platoon of B Company was placed as a perimeter guard around a small stone building. This building served as the company command post (CP). The other two platoons were dug in forward of the building.

Jimmy Burns huddled underneath a window of the building with one of the squad members they called Streaky. Jimmy and Streaky were serving as messengers to relay information from the company commander when so ordered. Streaky was tall and thin, with a voice that seemed to complain each time he spoke. He also spoke in a tone of arrogance that implied that he was a *tough guy*. Like many of the draftees who were still privates, he was lazy, having no intention of asserting himself as a soldier. He was there because he had to be, no other reason. Streaky had been a card dealer in an illegal gambling house prior to entering the service. He had mixed with criminals and *con men*, had seen plenty of hand guns, but no one had ever tried to shoot him before. Naturally, Streaky was afraid that night and kept questioning Jimmy Burns about the *odds* of living through a war.

"Do you really think we can win this war?" he asked Jimmy Burns.

"Of course," replied Jimmy Burns. "The Army wouldn't even have planned this invasion if they didn't think it would succeed."

"How long do you think the war will last?" asked Streaky.

"About a month," replied Jimmy Burns.

Many months later, Streaky was still reminding Jimmy Burns about the conversation they had that night. He delighted in telling Jimmy how "full of crap" that prediction turned out to be.

That night, Jimmy Burns could hear officers and his platoon sergeant talking inside the building. The company radio operator was tapping out messages in Morse code every few minutes.

The next morning the operator emerged bleary eyed from the building, advising Jimmy Burns, "We couldn't contact either of the other two companies or the battalion CP. Evidently they are still out of range for our radio. Something must have gone wrong over there on Omaha Beach."

Company B then moved cautiously along a causeway toward the town of Ste.-Mère-Eglise. Along the way they saw many dead soldiers lying on the edge of the road, both German and American. The causeway was narrow, barely wide enough for a vehicle to travel on, with waist deep swamps on either side of the roadway. At times the men of the 299th had to step aside and into the water to let columns of German prisoners pass, along with their paratrooper escorts, on the way back to the beach.

A few of the men were left at a small wooden bridge, to repair it as best they could without having any supplies with which to do the job.

The rest of the company moved on through Ste.-Mère-Eglise, southward on the road to Carentan, where they dug in with the paratroopers guarding the town against counter attack by the Germans. They spent an uneasy night there in ditches, as sporadic fighting continued all around them.

German snipers were discovered in houses and barns in the adjoining fields. These had to be dealt with one at a time by a squad or two of Company B men, usually led by a sharpshooting paratrooper of the 82nd Airborne Division.

The next day, the 299th men proceeded down the road in

the direction of Carentan. Heavy fighting was still in progress around Carentan; the city had not yet been captured. This situation would prevail for several more days.

Near a small village called Ste. Come-du-Mont, the engineers prepared several bridges for demolition, removed minefields, and served as infantry soldiers for seven days.

They salvaged the remnants of a destroyed wooden bridge, then rebuilt it so that a temporary bridge could be removed and sent forward to aid in the attack on Carentan. All this was done under heavy shelling by German artillery.

While at Ste. Come-du-Mont, the other two companies of the 299th arrived, having fought their way over from Omaha Beach in equally hazardous conditions. When Carentan finally fell around the middle of June, the battalion was shifted northward once again and pursued the front lines in the battle for Cherbourg.

Their duties alternated between engineering tasks and infantry assignments. One such infantry assignment involved the guarding of a large ammunition storage field, which duties were taken over from the infantry company in the middle of the night.

Once again Jimmy Burns found himself paired with a very nervous Streaky, who kept asking all night why they had to guard a place where American soldiers and trucks kept entering and leaving throughout the night. He was also concerned about the stench that was obvious to anyone that came close to where the two had positioned themselves at the entrance to the field. In the morning they found three bloated German bodies within an arm length of where they had spent that night.

Once again Streaky questioned Jimmy Burns about the prospects of ever surviving the war. Jimmy tried to reassure Streaky that it would soon be all over.

The 299th finally wound up in the vicinity of Orglandes where they were joined by the rear echelon with all their vehicles and equipment. The unit then moved back down to

Carentan, which turned out to be only a pile of rubble. Only foot soldiers and reconnaissance vehicles could make their way through the city.

The 299th now had their construction equipment and proceeded to build a by-pass road around Carentan. This job was interrupted from time to time by German shelling of bridges which had to be built and rebuilt over and over again.

Some time during this period a three-day storm brought the war to a virtual halt. The thunder and lightning was so severe that the noise and flash of guns seemed mild by comparison. Many years later, Jimmy Burns would remember this storm and only smile politely whenever friends or family would comment on the severity of a local thunderstorm.

While huddled soaking wet in a foxhole, shivering with fear of the lightning, Jimmy Burns thought about his Uncle Tip and Sergeant Eddie Boyd. He decided that no one was brave enough to go through this storm without being afraid. The more important question at the moment was bravery in battle. Jimmy Burns decided that he adapted very well to the dangers of war. Everyone was afraid, of course, but he found he was able to calm others such as Streaky when necessary. Even his Uncle Tip would have to admit that Jimmy Burns showed leadership qualities. Someday he would become an officer.

Chapter III

HOVELANGE

After the Normandy campaign, it seemed they were always moving to catch up to the front, pausing briefly to repair, build, or demolish bridges as they went along. Except for a couple of buzz bombs near Liege, Belgium, and another close call in Aachen, Germany, they thought that probably their combat days were in the past. After all, the battalion had been shifted away from the battle lines of First Army all the way back into Belgium.

For almost two months the battalion was spread all over Luxembourg and eastern Belgium, operating sawmills which provided lumber for First Army barracks construction. Only a squad or two worked at any one location.

Jimmy Burns and his squad were at a small mill in a little town called Hovelange, Luxembourg. Except for the crews that showed up weekly to haul away finished lumber, they seldom saw anyone from their own platoon. The platoon lieutenant, along with his driver, showed up periodically, and the company mess truck came by with rations once a week.

The squad was split into two shifts. Rod, the squad leader, handled the day shift. Jimmy Burns supervised the night shift, with the civilian mill owner overseeing the entire operation.

The squad was billeted in a bowling alley which was

located in a separate room of a small cafe. The men slept on the floor in their bedrolls, used the outdoor toilets behind the building, and got water from the bowling alley owner's home which adjoined the cafe. Between the two shifts, the sawmill operated about eighteen to twenty hours each day. During time-off periods, the men were free to roam the village on foot, or to drink beer and cognac at the local hotel. The village was little more than a crossroads; therefore, most of the off-duty time was spent at the hotel.

"What would Uncle Tip think of this assignment?" wondered Jimmy Buns.

"That's not soldiering," he would probably say. "Get yourself transferred to the infantry where the fighting occurs. You'll never become a solider in the rear echelon."

Luxembourg is a very beautiful country situated in a wooded and hilly section of the Ardennes Forest. Its boundaries touch Germany, Belgium, and France. A fiercely independent nation, Luxembourg is unwilling to call any one of those countries a benefactor, or even admit that its people might have descended from one of them.

Jimmy Burns learned of this after he became quite friendly with the hotel owner in Hovelange, a man named Nicholas Berthelemy. Nicholas spoke excellent English, as well as French, German, and his native language, which he called Letzeburghese. At first Jimmy thought—like most of the GIs—that these people were German. The language sure sounded like German; all the signs around town were posted in both German and French. For instance, at the train station a big sign read *Hovelange Gare/Hovelingen Bahnhof*. *Gare* means train station in French; likewise, *bahnhof* means the same thing in German.

Nicholas proved to be invaluable as a source of information to Jimmy Burns, and Jimmy's French improved as a result of their many conversations. Nicholas even taught him some German, which he claimed was quite distinct from Letzeburghese. The two languages always sounded about the same to Jimmy Burns.

Nicholas repeatedly insisted that there was no connection between Luxembourg and Germany—even though many wars had been fought on Luxembourg soil, and the country had been occupied by Germany on several occasions. He pointed out that the remote location of Hovelange had caused it to be spared from destruction during this war. The Germans did pass through the town during their recent occupation, and thus, there were some people in town that he would consider to be German collaborators.

Nicholas did not openly criticize anyone. He did, however, advise Jimmy Burns to be careful in dealing with some of them, including the lady that owned the bowling alley where they were billeted and the owner of the sawmill where they worked. Nicholas was an older man, and therefore, one of the few men still remaining in the town. All males sixteen to forty years of age had been either conscripted into the German army or otherwise relocated to Germany to work in factories.

Jimmy could hear his Uncle Tip say, "Stop fraternizing with the goddamn krauts."

Nicholas introduced Jimmy to a family who could be trusted, named Bovary. This introduction was the beginning of a friendship that developed between Jimmy and the Bovary family. The family was somehow related to Nicholas. Like many other families in the town, only the mother and two daughters remained, as their father and a brother had been whisked off to Germany with the rest. The family still lived in an apartment upstairs over the train station (Mr. Bovary had been the station master in Hovelange.) Mrs. Bovary performed the station duties for the few trains that ran through Hovelange between Luxembourg City and the other small towns further north.

Very few passengers got on or off in Hovelange. One in particular interested Jimmy Burns: Jeanne Bovary, the oldest Bovary daughter. Jeanne commuted weekly to work in Luxembourg City, coming home weekends only.

She was a very pretty girl, about eighteen years old. Her long blonde hair was always brushed or combed in a neat, orderly fashion. Her blue eyes seemed to radiate happiness, even though her young life had been filled with sad events. Jimmy spent a good deal of time with her on weekends.

There was little to do in the small town. They took long walks or sat on the station platform and talked. Conversation was difficult at first, because Jeanne did not speak English very well, and Jimmy's French and German phrases did not apply to the topics that young people discuss when they first meet. A younger sister, Elaine, was much more fluent in English; Mrs Bovary always made sure that Elaine went along with them on their walks, both to interpret and to make sure that the young American did not take advantage of Jeanne's innocence. They seemed to like each other well enough to become lovers, but on the few occasions that they found themselves alone, they always stopped just short of intimate sex.

Jimmy Burns had always been considered handsome by girls that he had met, but he was very shy and awkward when it came to sexual matters. He had been raised in an Irish-Catholic family, and the fear of mortal sin was always present whenever he considered *going all the way* with a girl. Furthermore, a Catholic chaplain in Normandy had advised him during confession to be especially careful, because the opportunities to sin would be many, but in a war zone the possibility of death was ever present. All good Catholics have a tremendous fear of arriving at the gates of heaven in a state of mortal sin. The other members of his squad envied him for having the prettiest girl in the town and kidded him about it constantly.

Jeanne Bovary was probably a virgin; at least she seemed to act like one around Jimmy Burns most of the time. Whenever he was inclined to forget the chaplain's warning, she always reminded him that they were both Catholic, and that the Church forbade sexual intercourse prior to marriage.

One Friday morning, Jimmy Burns walked down to the train station to visit the Bovary family and to inquire about Jeanne's arrival time for the weekend. He found Jeanne at home alone busily cleaning the apartment. Communication, as usual, was difficult, and Jimmy could neither determine why Jeanne was at home on a work day nor where her mother and sister were. He assumed they had gone shopping and would be home soon. After having a cup of hot chocolate with Jeanne, he left to meet with the lieutenant and the kitchen truck that was due to arrive with the weekly rations.

Sometime later he learned from Jeanne that she had been trying to tell him that her mother and Elaine had left for the day. Jeanne had taken a day off from work to take care of the station duties in her mother's absence. She also told him that she had hoped he would be making the usual advances that day because she had decided to give in to his wishes. Such an opportunity never presented itself again. Jimmy Burns thought about this day many times after he had left Hovelange for good.

Eventually, with the help of Elaine, Jimmy and Jeanne worked out the language barrier and talked a lot about their different childhoods, their dreams, and their hopes for the future. She told him about the local boy that she intended to marry, if and when he returned from his duty as a conscripted German soldier. Her boyfriend had only been gone about one year. From letters received, she knew that he was not in a front line unit, but did not know exactly where he was serving. Jimmy Burns told her about his high school sweetheart, and how he also hoped she would be waiting for him when he returned home.

Young Elaine was a typical twelve year old: enthusiastic and bubbly about everything, including the growing romance between Jeanne and Jimmy. She was always

26

encouraging them to hold hands and asked them to kiss, so that she could watch to learn how to do it. Secretly, Elaine told Jimmy that she was hoping that he would forget Jeanne and return to marry her after the war, when she had grown up. Not so secretly, she had told others, including Nicholas, that she was going to be Jimmy's wife. She even asked for Jimmy's home address so that she could look for him in the United States after the war.

Jimmy enjoyed some fine meals at the Bovary apartment and also some prepared by Nicholas' wife at the hotel. They were far superior to the army rations that he was accustomed to eating. He repaid their kindness with cigarettes for Nicholas and chocolate for the Bovary girls. Both Mr. Bovary and Nicholas' wife appreciated the sugar and coffee he was able to save for them from his rations. All this added up to very pleasant duty for one GI, named Corporal Jimmy Burns.

Probably Uncle Tip wouldn't approve of this kind of duty for Jimmy Burns.

"To hell with Uncle Tip," thought Jimmy Burns. Tip must have had some girl friends overseas. He had served in Mexico, France, China, and even Russia.

Down at the sawmill it was a different story. Jimmy Burns did not get along well with the owner, Joseph Waxweiler, from the first day that Jimmy had entered the mill. Even before he had talked with Nicholas at the hotel, Jimmy was suspicious of Joseph Waxweiler because Waxweiler looked, talked, and acted like a German. He was a small man with a round face, and wore a typical German moustache which strongly resembled Adolph Hitler's. Because of his appearance and the violent gestures he used when he was scolding them, the GIs all referred to Waxweiler as *Hitler* behind his back. He used the word *dumpkof* (the German word for stupid) frequently. He had plenty of reason to do so at first, because none of the Americans had ever been inside a sawmill, much less operate one.

Joseph Waxweiler was a bachelor. He lived with his younger sister Gerta, who served as his housekeeper and handled the bookkeeping chores for the sawmill. This was the story that everyone in town related, although no one could recall ever having talked to either Waxweiler, except for a casual greeting when passing in the street. The pair stayed pretty much to themselves. Apparently, they had no friends in town. It was obvious they were suspect, as evidenced by the raised eyebrows whenever Jimmy Burns sought more information about either Waxweiler.

As a shift supervisor, it was necessary for Jimmy to learn from Joseph how everything at the mill operated. Because Joseph spoke very little English, many of his instructions were simple hand signals with the expression "like so" being uttered from time to time. In addition to supervising the other men, Jimmy had to operate the big band saw, which was capable of causing the most damage if anything went wrong.

As luck would have it, the first time that Jimmy took control of the saw he ruined a saw blade. It was the result of his having shifted the feed mechanism mistakenly. He had meant to push the button which would return the carriage automatically at the end of the first cut. Joseph had started the cut for him, but had not explained what Jimmy was supposed to do at the end of the cut. Joseph immediately fell into a rage, the first of many that were to follow each time any of the men goofed. He became very upset if the error meant he would have to remove the saw blade to sharpen or straighten it.

Joseph Waxweiler resented the Americans taking over his sawmill. Both Jimmy Burns and Sergeant Rod had been warned about Joseph's attitude by their lieutenant, who had negotiated with Joseph for use of the mill (or, more correctly, had ordered him to make it available to the Army). The Army paid well for the lumber it took. Money was not the problem. Apparently, orders were to saw up *all* available logs at the mill. Joseph contended that some logs were choice hardwoods, protected by government regulations and were earmarked for extended seasoning. The American Army, as liberators, contended, just as the Germans before them probably had, that they wanted lumber, and lumber they were going to get, even if it meant cutting down the whole damn forest. Joseph prevailed, at least in part, because the squad worked their way around one particular pile of logs. One day a convoy of American trucks showed up with loads of logs from some other location.

Joseph was the only person capable of keeping the saw blades sharpened, and at first he spent the better part of both shifts at the mill. He barely took time to eat or to sleep; this may have accounted for him being so cross and irritable most of the time.

Lack of experience resulted in both supervisors dulling and bending numerous saw blades. These accidents sent Joseph into a violent rage each time that one occurred. The novice operators frequently hit nails, stones, and hard spots due to lack of experience. As well, some good logs were ruined by poor positioning or improper clamping. Gradually, however, the men began operating the equipment smoothly enough to please Joseph somewhat. The supervisors even trained a few other men to operate the saw, so that jobs could be traded from time to time. Sawing could become boring after a few hours; therefore, everyone welcomed the opportunity to take on different jobs.

Joseph became a bit friendly after a while, and one day took Jimmy Burns aside to apologize for his earlier behavior. Then he proceeded to teach him how to sharpen the big band saw blades on a machine that was very tricky to set up. The sawmill was quite old fashioned, but the machinery had been well maintained; therefore, production soared once the men learned to operate it correctly. Finished lumber output was outstanding. Joseph's bankbook surely reflected this, and was probably the main reason that he finally warmed up to them and became friendly.

Joseph's sister, Gerta, had always been friendly to the GIs. (Possibly this was another reason for his earlier mistrust and rude treatment of the Americans.) It was getting close to Thanksgiving Day, when Gerta suddenly announced that she would like to cook a big meal for the entire squad to be served on the following Saturday night. Both shifts were shortened that day, and at approximately six o'clock in the evening everyone sat down to what looked like an authentic American Thanksgiving dinner.

Everything was on the table except the traditional American Thanksgiving turkey; in its place was a big fat goose. When the GIs demolished the first goose, Gerta surprised them by bringing on a second one so that no one would leave hungry.

Joseph brought up wine from his cellar, as well as beer, cognac, and homemade *schnapps*. The latter proved to be high in alcoholic content, therefore very potent. The dinner turned into a drinking party, and everyone got pretty well smashed, including Joseph, who repeatedly offered toasts to the American Army and their forthcoming victory over Germany. The party continued late into the night, and became quite noisy when the GIs tried to teach Joseph and Gerta the raunchy songs they sang on occasions such as this.

Gerta had only drunk a little bit of wine, but was definitely in a party mood. She suddenly decided to sit on the lap of one of the GIs, and thanked him for liberating them by giving him a big, long kiss. She moved from lap to lap repeating the process with each of the men. She was quite a bit older than the oldest man there, not a beauty, being somewhat on the plump side. Nevertheless, she was female, and most of the men had not been this close to a woman in a long time.

It was quite dark in the room, which was lit only by

candlelight. Joseph was not aware of what was going on, because he had slipped into a drunken stupor. Gerta must have been suffering from the same lack of companionship as the guests, because she positioned herself on each lap in a way that encouraged the GIs to give her a quick feel as she kissed them. Later they found out in talking about it, that she had actually put her hand on a few guys' crotches, and whispered, "Oo la la," when she discovered that she had, indeed, aroused the male instinct in them.

She had worked her way half way around the table when she reached the lap of Sergeant Rod, and she stayed there for a long time. Whatever he was doing to her seemed to please her, for she did not seem to be in any hurry to leave.

Joseph suddenly came to, staggered to the end of the table, and pulled her from Sergeant Rod's lap, at the same time shouting for everyone to leave. The party was definitely over!

The soldiers all had trouble getting into the truck, and again, getting out of it at their billet, where they noisily stumbled into bed. The next day was a lost cause because the schnapps had a devastating effect on everyone, including Jimmy Burns, even though he had drunk mostly beer. He did not like either cognac or schnapps and rarely finished a shot glass of either drink.

It was almost noon when Rod awakened Jimmy Burns and asked him to help get the day crew awake and down to the mill. Some of the squad could not be roused, and those who were able to wake up were deathly sick from hangover. Jimmy and Rod managed to get up four men and walked them to the sawmill, which was about a mile and a half away.

Jimmy Burns went with them because he had dulled a saw blade on the last log that had been put through the saw the night before, and he had promised to sharpen it the first thing in the morning. Joseph was not around, so they set about preparing to saw lumber, as best they could, even though neither of them felt very good.

Jimmy Burns was showing Rod how to set up the saw blade on the sharpening machine when the lieutenant suddenly arrived and asked to see yesterday's production figures. A daily log of the number of board feet of lumber produced was kept, as well as a record of the size and number of logs used. Joseph usually kept track of this, because neither Rod nor Jimmy Burns knew how to calculate board feet of lumber.

The previous day's production was, of course, quite low due to the shortened shifts, and nothing had yet been entered for this day, even though the mill should have been operating almost six hours by now. Rod tried to bluff the lieutenant with tales of breakdowns, sickness among the squad, etc., but the lieutenant saw right through all this, and proceeded to read the riot act. He looked around for the other two men who should have been there as part of Rod's shift, then drove to the bowling lanes and got everyone out of their bedrolls. After threatening to court martial all of them, he made everyone report to the mill, where he stayed with them for the next twelve hours while the entire squad worked, with only a short break to eat around six o'clock that evening.

The lieutenant chewed out Joseph mercilessly, threatening to withhold his payments if such a thing ever happened again. With the entire squad working for twelve hours, lumber output was greater than it had ever been before. Every last piece of scrap was converted to finished lumber, and the mill never looked cleaner. The squad was exhausted, of course, and they were all very happy to return to their bedrolls that night.

After the party event, Joseph returned to his old, nasty ways, using abusive language to correct the men. He continued to blame the men for Gerta's behavior at the party.

The lieutenant started to show up at the mill more

frequently, and from then on what had been pleasant duty turned into a routine of drudgery. The members of the squad still continued to enjoy time off at the hotel, but no longer approached their jobs at the mill with the enthusiasm that they once had shown.

People in the town of Hovelange still treated the Americans in a friendly manner, but invitations to dinner seemed to become less frequent. The incident at the mill became known to everyone in town, and the Americans gained a reputation as rowdies. Families who had daughters were less inclined to have the Americans in their homes. Jimmy Burns had a difficult time convincing Nicholas and the Bovary family that the whole affair was quite innocent, being brought on primarily by the abundance of schnapps provided by Joseph Waxweiler. Exactly how the story got spread around town was something of a mystery. Possibly the men talked too freely about the party among themselves, even exaggerating some of the events. Life in Hovelange went on as before, but nothing again would occur to top the party for excitement.

Jimmy Burns chuckled, as once again he thought about the reaction his Uncle Tip would have to this phase of his stay in Hovelange. He would probably say, "Who ever heard of building barracks for soldiers right in the middle of a war? How can you win a war when everyone is fraternizing with the enemy?"

Sergeant Eddie Boyd would have been more considerate, complimenting Jimmy Burns on his ability to resist getting drunk with the others. He always said, "Good soldiers never drink enough to let it affect their duty."

These thoughts slowly gave way to another event that occurred during the stay in Hovelange—an event that would change forever Jimmy Burns' viewpoint on Army duty and his desire to become an officer.

Chapter IV

THE BRIDGE

On the fifteenth of December, Burns and his crew left the mill about midnight as usual. They stopped by the hotel for a nightcap with Nicholas, the owner, who always waited up for them even though he had no other customers. They entered into the usual discussion with him about the war. Nicholas kept them up to date on the Allies' progress by listening to the BBC broadcasts every night. That night the news was particularly encouraging with the report of an Allied offensive underway. Surely this would split the German defenses, and bring about an early end to the war.

At one o'clock they walked the short distance to the bowling alley and climbed into their bedrolls for what they expected to be a good night's sleep, before having to go back to the mill for their next shift.

It seemed to Burns that he had barely turned in, when he was awakened and scrambled outside with everyone else to see what all the noise was about. The men were none too quiet themselves, as they stumbled half dressed in unlaced boots through the cafe and out the front door. The sky to the northeast was illuminated by what appeared to be a huge thunderstorm. They quickly recognized the storm as the noise and flash of heavy artillery fire. Everyone was amazed at the intensity of the light and loudness of the firing, because it was taking place nearly twenty-five miles away.

While they were discussing the possibilities, the lieutenant showed up in his jeep and ordered them to pack the truck and report to the company CP. During the ride back to the CP, Jimmy Burns tried to reassure the squad that they were probably going to play infantry again as a backup to the big push Nicholas had heard about on the BBC.

That afternoon he was to learn differently. The squad was sent out to a small crossroads to load an earthen bridge with demolitions, and to stand by to blow it, if and when the Germans approached with tanks. They were also instructed to defend the bridge against infantry attack, and blow it only if the enemy attacked with overwhelming numbers. It seemed the German army had gone on the offensive and had broken through the American defenses in an attempt to capture Bastogne, approximately five miles north of the bridge they were to defend.

Part of the squad quickly placed demolitions, camouflaged the truck with its fifty-caliber machine gun, placed a thirty-caliber machine gun to protect the right flank of the bridge, and put sentries in foxholes at the entrance to the bridge. The rest of the squad dug foxholes halfway between the bridge and the truck on both sides of the road that ran down to the bridge.

The electric detonator wires, as well as the backup fuzes, were connected to the demolitions. The detonator was placed in Jimmy Burns' foxhole, next to the rear of the truck. Sergeant Rod had a foxhole nearby, which enabled either man to stand watch over the detonator at all times. One wire was always disconnected from the detonator for safety reasons. At the last minute prior to firing, this final connection had to be carefully made before pushing the plunger of the detonator. This was the most important step in the entire procedure.

The fifty-caliber machine gun—their main weapon—was attached to the truck on an anti-aircraft mounting. This mounting was connected to the truck rack immediately behind the cab on the right hand side. The gun was clamped to a circular metal frame. The clamp could move around the frame, so that the gunner was able to stand inside the metal frame and fire the gun in any direction. The gun could tilt upward to the sky to fire at low flying aircraft, but could not point down below a position slightly above horizontal. It was ideally suited to this mission. The truck sat slightly tilted to the right facing the road for a quick getaway. From this vantage point, the fifty-caliber gun could be fired over the bridge at the approaching enemy without danger of firing accidentally at the bridge. Also, this gun could pivot left or right to provide covering fire when the truck took off after the bridge had been blown.

The thirty-caliber machine gun was mounted on a tripod and had to be carefully positioned where it could be most effective, and in a position that best protected the gunner from enemy fire. Once in place, it could not be easily moved without being disassembled and repositioned. This gun was placed about half way up the hill on the right side of the bridge to cover an open field, should enemy infantry-men try to cross the stream from that direction. Only a couple of riflemen were positioned alongside the thirty-caliber, the largest number of riflemen dug in on the left side of the bridge to protect that area against infantry approach to the stream.

These preparations were completed by midnight on the sixteenth of December; for the next three days this position was held waiting for something to happen. The lieutenant stopped by several times to bring the men rations, as well as to inspect the position they were holding. A major from the battalion came by once and ordered the thirty-caliber machine gun replacement changed, as well as relocation of some of the riflemen. This was done because intelligence data the major had received indicated the attack, when it came, would probably consist of a lone tank or two backed up by a substantial force of infantrymen. Therefore, two bazookas were issued to the forward sentry positions, and an anti-tank gun with crew was promised just as soon as one could be spared.

The bazooka was an anti-tank weapon which resembled a piece of a small diameter stovepipe. Officially, it was a 2.75 inch anti-tank rocket launcher. Because of its similarity to an unusual musical instrument popularized by comedian Bob Burns, the weapon had been nicknamed *bazooka*.

The bazooka was powerful enough to destroy armored reconnaissance vehicles; however, against the thick front armor of a tank it was ineffective. The best way to use it against a tank was to hit the rear of the tank, where the armor was not as thick, or to hit the tank tread wheels. The tank could not steer or turn with damaged tread wheels. A lucky shot just below the turret of a tank might disable the turret turning mechanism, forcing it to change its firing direction by steering the tank around with the tread drive. This made the tank a sitting duck for anti-tank weapons, and it would usually retreat once it lost its maneuverability.

Once the bazooka man fired this device, his position was immediately revealed. Getting off a second shot was difficult. A shot at the rear of a tank was almost impossible, so the best one could hope for was a disabling hit at the treads or turret line. All of the squad members had test-fired the bazooka, but no one had proved to be proficient with this weapon.

Darkness was falling on the nineteenth of December, when a caravan of horse-drawn wagons came rolling down the road and pulled into a farmyard just north of the bridge. The wagons contained civilian refugees with all the possessions they could manage to get aboard. These people were trying to escape the battle which had already driven them out of their homes. Their leader conferred with Sergeant Rod about when the bridge was going to be blown. He asked Rod to let him know ahead of time in order that their group might cross the bridge while it was still standing. As much as Rod hoped he could accommodate these people, he knew full well that the bridge had to be blown as soon as an enemy tank attempted to gain access to it.

It was learned from the civilian refugees that the battle extended a long way from their present position. The caravan had travelled just over thirty miles, taking a circuitous route from Clervaux, Luxembourg, located well north and east of Bastogne. The German army had rolled up the American defensive positions with devastating tank and artillery fire. Because the refugees had witnessed brutal killing of civilians by German soldiers, they had gathered up whatever possessions they could to try to escape the carnage. Sergeant Rod assured the leader of the group that he would make every effort to notify them if orders were received to blow the bridge before dawn.

A lieutenant from the 28th Infantry Division came along in the middle of the night, advising that a ring of armor existed around Bastogne and that German tanks were right behind him heading toward the bridge. The lieutenant was all alone, having been with the last defenders at Wiltz, Luxembourg, which had been division headquarters for the 28th Division.

"Why not blow the bridge now and get out of here?" the lieutenant asked Sergeant Rod.

"No, my instructions are to defend the bridge until we are attacked," answered Rod.

"You're gonna have to blow it sooner or later. I could order you to do it now, you know," said the lieutenant.

"I only take orders from my own officers," Rod responded.

The lieutenant's voice seemed to break up as he continued to argue with Sergeant Rod. He was obviously scared and did not want to set out on his journey alone again.

Jimmy Burns remembered a conversation he had with his

Uncle Tip many years ago.

"What are you going to be when you grow up?" Tip had asked.

"An officer in the Army," had been the reply.

"Officers are no goddamned good. Be a sergeant; they run the Army. All officers do is sign a lot of papers made out by sergeants," Tip advised.

Seeing the lieutenant from the 28th so frustrated by his situation made Jimmy Burns wonder if perhaps Uncle Tip wasn't right after all.

Ever since the sixteenth of December, when this episode had started, the men of the squad had heard tanks, artillery, and rifle fire in all directions except behind them. They also heard other noises that they recognized: the loud thud of demolitions blowing up bridges. These sounds were evidently the work of other members of the battalion manning similar barriers in the region.

The bridge that Burns and his group were defending was located on a remote road; hence, they would not be tested until the main roads had all been denied to the Germans. They had an almost perfect defensive position set up, having placed the camouflaged truck with the fifty-caliber behind a grove of trees next to the road that sloped gently down to the bridge. Beyond the bridge, the road continued downhill for about fifty yards, then ran uphill and curved out of sight behind a large tree which stood next to a group of farm buildings. If they had received that anti-tank gun, the squad could have kept a tank coming around that corner at bay almost indefinitely. Of course, if a large number of infantrymen accompanied the tank, the position would have been overrun eventually. Other than their rifles, the only weapons the squad had were the two machine guns and the two bazookas.

The lieutenant from the 28th Division was absolutely right when he predicted that German tanks would soon be coming down this little road. Just before dawn the first one came clanking along and stuck his nose out from behind the big tree. It was still dark, but the shape of the tank stood out clearly to the men at the bridge. Their eyes had become adjusted to the dark, after having spent three nights peering into the darkness. The fifty-caliber machine gun opened up immediately, firing at and scattering the infantrymen who were riding on the German tank. The two bazookas fired almost simultaneously, both missing because the tank was well out of range. After firing the bazookas, the two sentries on the far side of the bridge retreated to foxholes on the near side of the bridge. The thirty-caliber machine gun proved ineffective, because it had been moved too close to the bridge on the right hand side.

The German infantrymen wisely opted to take cover behind the big tree and the farm buildings which were to the left side of the bridge.

The thirty-caliber gunner opened fire, but found he could only shoot in a high arc over the bridge, and could not hit anything except the upper branches of the trees. The fifty-caliber machine gun continued to fire, but only bounced bullets off the tank, which by this time had closed the protective hatches.

The tank backed up a short distance until most of it was hidden by the big tree, and sat there for several minutes. The tank commander was, evidently, trying to assess the strength of the group that he was facing. This delay provided the time necessary to get all of the squad away from the bridge and into the truck. The tank commander soon realized that he had little to fear from this small group of defenders. He maneuvered the tank around the tree and started for the bridge with machine guns blazing. The tank's big cannon was poised to destroy everything in sight, as soon as it could get on the upslope toward the bridge.

Jimmy Burns thought time had come to a standstill as he fumbled with the loose detonator wire, trying to connect it to its terminal. His hands were numb with cold and his fingers seemed to lack the necessary strength to complete the connection. Finally, he pushed the detonator plunger down and jumped on the truck with the others. The bridge went up with a tremendous roar. The tank had managed to fire a couple of rounds, but they passed harmlessly overhead. The truck took off (with debris from the bridge explosion falling all over it), slowly climbed to the crest of the hill, raced down the other side to the main road, and back to the company CP.

Nobody looked back, but the tank must also have been covered with dirt, stone, and mud. It was almost on the bridge when the charge went off. The plan had been to blow the bridge just as the tank reached the middle of it, but this was a small bridge. If the main detonator had failed, there would not have been time to activate the backup before the tank reached the other side of the bridge. Also, survival was important in order to be able to withdraw to another barrier line to the rear. The job of the engineers was to delay the enemy so that reinforcements could be organized and brought up to halt the advance permanently.

It was daylight when the squad arrived back at the company CP. There they met the company commander, a few officers, kitchen and supply people, drivers, radiomen, and two or three other squads. None of these men were from their own platoon.

After eating some breakfast rations, the squad was sent to an orchard behind the CP to dig in and get some rest. They had no trouble falling asleep, for most of them had not closed their eyes since December fifteenth, almost five days ago.

Jimmy Burns wondered what would happen to the civilian refugees trapped in the farmhouse on the other side of the bridge. He also wondered what had happened to the lieutenant from the 28th Division, whom he did not recall seeing in the truck when it had arrived at the company CP.

Before drifting off to sleep, Jimmy Burns thought some more about whether or not he really wanted to become an officer. Maybe the strain of battle was more severe on officers, as evidenced by that lieutenant from the 28th. Perhaps the fellow had been through a whole lot more than they realized. Uncle Tip had said that sergeants ran the Army. Sergeant Rod had sure taken control of this little battle. Anyway, Tip's experience had all been in World War I. His letters home always mentioned trenches and bayonet attacks. He could hardly comment on modern day warfare.

Sergeant Eddie Boyd would have been proud of what he saw the squad perform in the last few days. Jimmy Burns could remember the first time he had connected detonator wires with the help of Sergeant Eddie Boyd. He was sure that Eddie would continue to advise him to pursue a career as an officer.

Chapter V

TASK FORCE

It was dark again when the squad was awakened, given another meal of canned rations, and loaded into the squad truck. Not one of the men had the slightest idea of where they were going. This mission seemed to be highly secret and quite screwed up from the beginning. It started out in a column of three or four trucks, soon stopped, waited for what seemed like hours, returned to the CP, waited for awhile, then finally started out again.

In talking to members of the first platoon, it was learned that a bridge that had been blown earlier by them in a town called Martelange had not been completely destroyed. They were now heading down the same road which would take them to that bridge.

Occasionally, their supplies included defective explosives. As a result, no matter how well the explosives were placed, or what quantities were used, a bridge might remain in semi-operating condition after setting off the charge. This was not a problem if the bridge was being destroyed to clear if from the area, in order to replace it with another bridge. It could always be reloaded with more explosives and finished off. However, when blowing a bridge as a barrier defense—as in this case—with the enemy there, the bridge had to be recaptured first. This, evidently, Jimmy Burns decided, was most likely their mission that night.

They arrived at the edge of the town around midnight on foot, having left the trucks with all of their gear in another small town about five miles back. Corporal Burns and his squad leader, Sergeant Rod, along with all the other noncoms, were called to a meeting behind a small shack to the rear of where the column had been halted. There the noncoms were told that this group was a *task force*, with the mission of recapturing the town of Martelange and defending the partially destroyed bridge against enemy crossings. Earlier reconnaissance revealed that the bridge was still usable to light vehicles and infantry, even though a tank could probably not get across it.

In the dark, Jimmy Burns did not recognize all of the men there. He decided that some of the officers must be from other companies or headquarters staff.

He and Rod returned to their squad and told the men to spread out in the ditches alongside the road, as they had been instructed by the captain in charge of the task force.

A short time later, Burns was again called back to the rear of that same shack, which by now was identified as the task force CP. This task force had started out with Burns' own company commander in charge, a captain named Ambrose Marion. The men had always called him Blinkey, because of his habit of nervously blinking his eyes whenever he talked to anyone.

Captain Marion had been company commander of B Company from the very beginning, back in basic training when the battalion was first activated. He was disliked intensely by the men, who considered him to be a poor leader and the most chicken shit officer in the entire battalion. Their estimation of him had proved to be correct many times in the past, because of his cowardly behavior each time the company had been engaged in battle. Now was no exception.

When Burns arrived at the task force CP, he found that another captain named Stern was in charge. Captain Marion was still there, but was lying on the ground all covered up with other officers' coats. He was shivering and shaking with a conveniently contracted case of flu.

Burns recognized Captain Stern as someone he knew quite well, having had him as a platoon lieutenant, briefly, in basic training. He was regarded as a good officer, and one that the men would gladly follow into battle. Captain Stern had been transferred to the headquarters staff and was in charge of intelligence for the battalion. It was he who had determined that the bridge at Martelange was still partially standing. His original purpose on this mission had been as an adviser to Captain Marion.

"What a lucky break, to have Captain Stern take over the task force," thought Jimmy Burns, as he waited to talk to this captain, who was busy advising a lieutenant as to where he wanted some of the men located. Jimmy had a great fondness and admiration for Captain Stern, who had been responsible for Jimmy's promotion to corporal after only a few weeks of basic training.

Later, Captain Stern recommended that Jimmy be sent to a special training program, after which he was tested and interviewed for Officer Candidate School. At that time Burns was only nineteen years old. The minimum age for Officer Candidate School was twenty-one; however, the age limit could be waived if exceptional ability was evident. Jimmy failed to pass the test, but upon his return to the battalion, it was Captain Stern that counseled him on his shortcomings.

They met once more after that in Normandy, when Captain Stern showed up in B Company area one day and asked for Jimmy Burns, plus an interpreter nicknamed Frenchie, to go with him into a nearby village. Frenchie's real name was Armand Gregoire. He spoke excellent French because his parents were French-Canadian.

The three spent several hours questioning villagers relative to rank, insignia numbers, and location of Germans who had been living in the village prior to the invasion. Although Jimmy and Frenchie were never told the purpose or results of this mission, Jimmy felt good about Captain Stern having selected him for it.

During the jeep ride back, Captain Stern had, once again, talked to Jimmy about his career future, and advised him regarding what he must do to be promoted to sergeant. He also told him that he had asked Captain Marion to release Jimmy for transfer to the Intelligence Section. Captain Marion had refused, citing the present shortage of men in the company, and the fact that he needed some time to sort out replacements that were to arrive soon.

"Someday soon, I hope to have you with me full time as battalion intelligence sergeant," Captain Stern had said. "Intelligence experience will help you later on as you pursue an officer career in the Army."

As Captain Stern turned away from the lieutenant and greeted Jimmy Burns, the thought occurred to Jimmy that the captain must be terribly disappointed in him because he was still a corporal. Instead, Captain Stern seemed pleased to see him, and immediately told him that he had seen Jimmy's name on a promotion list that only required final approval by the battalion commander.

"After that it will only be a formality to have you transferred to my intelligence group. Do you still want the job?" asked Captain Stern.

"Yes, I sure do," replied Jimmy Burns.

Captain Stern went on to explain that he had selected Jimmy for a patrol assignment because he knew that he could depend on him to do a good job. He said that he had personally observed the German troop movements through the town that afternoon. As far as the captain could determine, no vehicles had crossed the bridge, and it was pretty well destroyed, but not completely. All tanks and heavy vehicles had been routed north, up the highway on the other side of the bridge. This road led directly to Bastogne.

46

Except for a few guards directing traffic, he did not believe that the Germans were occupying the town in force. The bridge actually separated the town into halves, with buildings being located on either side.

With Jimmy Burns holding a flashlight cupped between his two hands, the captain drew a small sketch of the town layout and told Jimmy to take a patrol into the town. He wanted a first-hand report of the bridge's condition and verification that more German troops had not moved into the town after he had left his observation position several hours ago.

He told Jimmy to sneak in quietly, and to avoid contact with German sentries, should any be posted on this side of the bridge. Burns was to make the patrol as quickly as possible and report back to the captain upon his return.

Jimmy left the CP and returned to the squad to select his *volunteers* for this assignment. Volunteering for anything was unheard of in most Army units, and it was kind of a joke to say that one was selecting volunteers to do something. Sure, the Marines, the Airborne, Commandos, Rangers, and certainly, many infantry divisions had true volunteers, but in most outfits, the old Army expression, "I want three volunteers: you, you, and you," prevailed.

He always selected Frenchie for something like this in case they should meet civilians along the way. Jimmy selected a couple of other men who seemed to be alert, then started down the road with them toward the bridge. The night was so dark that the patrol proceeded down the road almost huddled together. Wisps of fog swirled around the group of bodies as they moved along. They walked quietly, picking up their feet with every step to avoid making noise. They had gone less than a mile when they reached the bridge entrance without seeing anyone or hearing anything.

It was very dark, but Jimmy could make out the demolished sections of the bridge hanging down into what looked like a shallow creek. He motioned the other three to spread out and dropped to one knee with his rifle poised in readiness. The others took a similar stance, but moved to the right behind a stone wall that guarded the bridge entrance.

Jimmy Burns then waited a few minutes before stepping out onto the bridge abutment. When he touched an upright post, that section of the bridge seemed to sway, somewhat like a foot bridge suspended over a deep gorge that one often saw in a Tarzan movie.

He kicked hard at a loose board, and it went noisily tumbling down the bridge roadway into the water below. He quickly moved back to the stone wall and took cover with the rest of the patrol. He then waited to see what kind of response was going to come from the other side of the bridge.

After a couple of minutes of silence, he decided that any enemy on the other side would surely have been alerted. It was so quiet it was frightening. Jimmy started to whisper instructions to the rest, but found that his voice wouldn't function. Only a wheeze seemed to come out.

Deciding that the mission had been completed, he motioned to the others to follow and moved back out onto the road for the return trip.

They heard German voices coming from the other side of the river just as they reached the last house on the road out of the town. The patrol stopped for a moment to listen, but heard nothing further. Deciding the voices were those of traffic guards who were stationed some distance from the bridge, the patrol returned quietly back up the road to the starting point.

After dropping the other three men off, Burns went back to the CP to report his findings to Captain Stern. The captain seemed relieved that they had not seen or heard any Germans at the bridge and was satisfied with the assessment that the bridge was destroyed sufficiently to prevent tanks from crossing over it. He confirmed that traffic guards he had seen earlier were some distance from the bridge and would have taken some time to get to the bridge to investigate a noise.

He dismissed Burns with a comment like, "Well done," and Jimmy returned to where the rest of the squad was resting in a ditch alongside the road. Throughout the night, traffic noise could be heard coming from the direction of the town, including tanks—but everything seemed to be moving north toward Bastogne, exactly as the captain said he had observed during the daytime.

It was almost daylight when they received orders to move out of the ditches, and to walk slowly, but quietly, into the town. Again, the trip passed without incidence until they took up a position behind the same stone wall that Jimmy Burns and his patrol had hidden the night before.

Once in this position, they could see immediately that the enemy was, indeed, now on the other side of the bridge. Two large tanks were sitting on the opposite approach with their big guns pointing right at them.

Suddenly, all hell broke loose. The enemy tanks opened up with their big cannons and machine guns, tearing huge chunks out of the wall and the surrounding buildings.

The task force retreated back across the street behind a house that had a barn attached, with stables in the basement. Several attempts were made to position machine guns so as to keep enemy troops from crossing the bridge. A couple of bazooka rounds were fired at the tanks without success.

After what seemed like hours, some of the task force, including Jimmy Burns, wound up trapped in the stable of the barn, along with several cows. Captain Stern was alongside Jimmy in the stable, while his other officers and the rest of the group were spread around in the few buildings that were still standing on this side of the town.

The cows mooed incessantly; this battle had interrupted the milking process, which must have just about begun when the firing started. There were milk pails all about. One of them sat half full underneath the first cow in the stable, right next to the small window through which they had all entered.

The tank's guns fired constantly, leveling buildings closest to the bridge first, and then—finally—the upper level of the building where they were holed up. More and more of the task force men came into the stable, as gradually, they lost the protection of the buildings where they had sought refuge.

Finally, the shelling stopped, and soon thereafter German infantry appeared at the small window, each firing several rounds from automatic weapons into the stable. The cows mooed and groaned as bullet after bullet hit them with a loud *splat!*

The gunfire ceased periodically, at which time Jimmy Burns could hear German voices discussing the situation. He wondered why the Germans kept returning to the window demanding surrender. Later he would learn the Germans had good reason to suspect Americans were in the stable. Fortunately, sounds emanating from the cows prevented the Germans from hearing any noise the American soldiers made as they moved about seeking safer locations.

During one particularly long period without gunfire, the owner of the property walked in through the doorway of the stable. Upon seeing the Americans, he beat a hasty retreat back into the cellar of his home.

Staff Sergeant Hogar squeezed in between Jimmy Burns and Captain Stern to report that the only remaining men of the task force were now crammed into the stable. The others had surrendered when they were caught in the open, trying to get up to the road and out of town. Sergeant Hogar also reported the incident of the Belgian civilian entering the stable. Hogar told Captain Stern he thought the civilian would soon be reporting what he had seen to the

Germans. He also suggested that perhaps it was time to surrender.

"There goes my promotion and transfer," thought Jimmy Burns. He had spent most of last night thinking about how proud his Uncle Tip would be when he received the news of Jimmy's promotion. He had thought about Sergeant Eddie Boyd, too, and could hardly wait to get a letter off to him with the announcement. Now, he had to wonder what the two of them would think about his being captured. A lousy turn of events for a soldier that wanted to become an officer.

Chapter VI

CAPTURE

The cows continued to moo as they shifted their feet about in the straw beneath them. This was the only noise heard in the stable for several long minutes. There were only three cows and an equal number of empty stalls in the small stable. GIs occupied the empty stalls or lined the floor along the back wall of the little room. Captain Stern, Sergeant Hogar, and Jimmy Burns were in the stall farthest from the entrance window.

"It looks like we are going to have to surrender," Captain Stern whispered to Jimmy Burns. "It's only a matter of time before a grenade comes through that window."

"What should I do?" asked Jimmy Burns.

"First, pass the word that we are surrendering. Then take this white handkerchief to the window and wave it. Holler *komrad*, but don't stick your head out the window until you're sure they understand." replied the captain.

Jimmy Burns took the handkerchief and slid on his belly, backwards, out of the stall that he had been sharing with the captain and Sergeant Hogar. He rose to his knees just as another burst of fire from the Germans came through the window. The noise was deafening and had a numbing effect on Jimmy Burns. He jumped to his feet, rushed to the window, waved the handkerchief, and shouted hysterically, *"Komrad, komrad!"*

The German soldier who had been firing in through the window seemed surprised. He jumped back from the window and fired his machine-pistol aimlessly into the air.

The German said something that sounded like, "Come slowly, with hands up."

Jimmy Burns climbed out the window, and the rest of the group followed, one at a time. As they were being lined up alongside the farmhouse that adjoined the stable, Jimmy saw several American GI overcoats, including his own, piled at the foot of a German soldier. The German was going through the pockets of each coat and dumping out the contents: ammunition, food, candy, cigarettes, even personal letters.

Jimmy thought about the letter he had just received from his mother. He hadn't had time to read it carefully, but remembered some confusing information in it about his Uncle Tip losing his master sergeant's stripes.

The overcoats had been taken off by Burns and the rest of the men prior to entering the stable, so they could squeeze through the small window. The overcoats had tipped off the Germans to the fact that the Americans must be in the stable. This is why they kept firing in through the window.

A German soldier about fifteen years old started to offer an overcoat to Jimmy Burns when a German sergeant standing nearby began shouting and grabbed the overcoat from the young soldier. The German sergeant then pointed his machine-pistol at the pile of coats and fired a stream of bullets into the pile. It had started to snow lightly; Jimmy Burns knew he was going to miss the warmth of that big overcoat. Little did he know how serious a loss this would be when over the next few weeks he would suffer the most severe cold and misery of his young life.

The Germans marched their prisoners single file to the bridge, which proved to be strong enough to support foot soldiers, if not heavy vehicles. Crossing the bridge was difficult. One side sloped steeply into the water, which meant wet feet for everyone to get to the other side. The prisoners then had to scale a three-foot wall of the last pier before walking across that wobbly section.

A couple of German scout cars had already crossed over somehow, and were heading up the road toward the next town. The Americans had left vehicles in that town the night before. Jimmy Burns thought about the rest of his personal belongings which had been left with the squad truck. He wondered if the Germans would destroy the rest of his clothing as they had his overcoat.

It was late in the afternoon when the group of prisoners arrived on the other side of the bridge. The snowfall was increasing. The prisoners were lined up again, alongside other members of the task force who had surrendered earlier. The same surly German sergeant was shouting, *"Funf mann, funf mann."*

The German sergeant walked up and down the line of prisoners; finally stopping in front of Jimmy Burns, he asked gruffly, *"Kennen Deutch gesprachen?"* He also repeated in English, "Can you speak German?"

Jimmy Burns was scared to death, and kept shaking his head left to right to answer no.

The German sergeant kept badgering Jimmy Burns, as if he had singled him out because of the overcoat incident.

When the German sergeant said, *"Vous parlais Francais?"* Jimmy Burns blurted out, *"Une peu."*

With this utterance, Jimmy had broken the first basic rule of capture. A prisoner was only required to give his name, rank, and serial number to a captor. All other conversation was forbidden. The German then rattled off in French a whole string of phrases that Burns, truly, did not understand.

An American sergeant standing next to Burns then said out of the side of his mouth, "Keep your mouth shut."

Jimmy Burns finally ended the conversation with, *"Je nes*

comprend pas."

Shortly thereafter, the German sergeant was called by a German officer to look at a problem the Germans were having with an American tank. They must have captured it, or found it abandoned. It had been setting there when Burns and his group were marched across the bridge. A German soldier was up on the turret of the tank trying to fire a machine gun which was mounted there. The German sergeant stood next to the tank shouting instructions up to the German soldier in a critical tone of voice. The unfortunate German soldier could not get the gun to fire and seemed frustrated by all the instructions he was receiving, both from the sergeant and the German officer. He would pull the hammer back and press the trigger, but nothing happened. Every second time that he pulled the hammer back, a live round of ammunition would fly out and bounce off the side of the tank to the street below.

The German sergeant climbed up unto the tank and took over the job of trying to fire the gun. The sergeant kept shouting at the poor German soldier. The results were the same for the German sergeant, as round after round of live ammunition kept falling to the ground.

Another German soldier was busy picking up the fallen ammunition and stuffing them into his pockets. Soon, the German officer joined the other two on the tank turret, all three of them taking turns pulling back on the hammer without success.

The American prisoners were quite amused by all the shouting and arm waving that was going on. Even the German soldiers guarding the prisoners seemed to be enjoying this little scene and only smiled whenever an American would put his hand to his mouth to stifle laughter. It would be many long days before the prisoners would again see an incident as humorous as this one.

Later that night, Frenchie explained to Jimmy Burns what the Germans were doing wrong in their attempt to fire the gun. Frenchie had been to gunnery school and was familiar with this type of machine gun. It was a simple case of pulling the hammer back twice rapidly to negate a safety feature. The Germans did not understand this and never did get the gun to fire that day. The shouting could still be heard as the prisoners were marched down the street a short distance and locked in the cellar of a tavern.

Although they received no food that night, the German guards—most of whom appeared to be under eighteen years of age—did slip them pails of beer from the tavern above. The German soldiers not on guard duty must have been celebrating their victory; it was very noisy upstairs with singing and foot stomping. The music sounded like it was coming from either an accordion or a concertina.

Sitting there on the dirt floor of the cellar, Jimmy started to note who some of the other men were that had been captured with him. Although the cellar was dark, whenever the German guards entered with buckets of beer, they shined a flashlight around, and Jimmy could recognize most of the faces around him.

On the opposite side of the room, he could pick out others by their voices and decided that they were all from his company. Here, sitting in that cellar, was the complete task force from the night before, except for the officers, who must have been separated and were being held elsewhere.

His own squad was there, plus a squad from the first platoon, all of whom he knew quite well. The only platoon sergeant was Hogar from the third platoon, but none of his men were with him. Surprisingly, the company first sergeant was there in the cellar with the rest of them. This confirmed Jimmy's earlier suspicion that the task force had been hastily assembled for this mission.

Long periods of silence would be interrupted by a sudden outbreak of whispered conversation among the prisoners.

Jimmy Burns had not given much thought to what was

going to happen to them until he heard someone say, "If they were going to shoot us, they would have done it up there in the street."

Someone else said, "They will probably wait until morning when the light is better."

This statement sent a wave of fear throughout the cellar as everyone started talking at once. Nervous voices talked of escape and how to go about it.

Sitting next to Jimmy Burns, on one side, was Squad Sergeant Ray Coon; on the other side, Coon's assistant, Corporal Jim Kelsey. Burns knew Kelsey quite well because they had spent time together drinking beer while on passes, way back in basic training. Burns and Kelsey had received their corporal stripes on the same day, which was the beginning of their friendship, but they were not close buddies.

The little sleep they all got that night was in a sitting position, because there was not enough room to lie down. Kelsey and Burns slumped against each other's shoulders to try to keep warm, and slept as best they could.

The next morning, the prisoners were marched up a long hill on the east side of town, down the other side, and on to the next town. A road sign revealed that this town's name was Bigonville.

For the next few weeks, he would see road sign after road sign with town names he had never heard of, nor could he pronounce them.

They passed through Bigonville—or what was left of it—and were halted at a farm at the edge of the town. The prisoners were herded into a large shed that resembled a corn crib. Open space showed between the boards of this building, and the floor seemed to sag under their weight, as if the building was setting up on blocks without a foundation to support it.

There must have been other prisoners in the shed when they arrived, because they were now crammed into a space much too small for the number of prisoners present. A quick look around by Burns revealed that there could be as many as fifty men in the building.

The man next to him was a complete stranger who kept looking at a map that he constantly removed and replaced inside his shirt, next to his bare chest.

When Burns questioned the stranger, he simply whispered, "Twenty-eighth," and returned to his map reading.

Occasionally, he looked outside through the open space of the boards, as if he were looking for landmarks. Burns saw just enough of the map to recognize it as an American Army grid map, which he had become familiar with during map training sessions in basic training. Others in the building were having conversations, but Jimmy Burns learned little about this stranger.

A German officer suddenly stuck his head in the doorway of the shed and said in English, "If anyone in here is an American officer, please step forward at once."

Two or three of the prisoners worked their way out to the door, including the stranger whom Burns had been observing.

Later, Jimmy Burns wondered if perhaps that stranger and the others who left might have been Germans planted in their midst to gain information. He had told the stranger what outfit he was with. During interrogation later that night, Burns was sure that the stranger had relayed information to the Germans.

Interrogation—when it came—turned out to be nothing at all like Jimmy Burns had expected: a lone prisoner sitting in a chair under a bright light in an almost empty room with the interrogator blowing smoke in his face. Instead, they were led in a group through a hillside orchard to a farmhouse where they all stood around waiting, while one at a time, they were taken into the farmhouse.

It had continued snowing throughout the day, and several inches had piled up on the ground. Jimmy Burns stood there, shivering, without his overcoat. He did have on his field jacket, a wool sweater, and wool shirt and pants, along with his long underwear. He had his wool knit cap and helmet liner, but not the steel helmet; the Germans had taken it from him.

When his turn finally came, he was escorted into the house through a back door, down a long hallway, and into the dining room. The warm air and the smell of food caused a good feeling to ripple through his cold and weary body.

A table in the middle of the room showed evidence of a leisurely meal having been consumed recently. Dirty dishes, glassware, serving bowls, and silverware still cluttered the table. Except for the carcass of a goose, there was not any food left on the table. Empty wine bottles indicated that a group of about twelve people had enjoyed themselves while the prisoners were standing outside cold and hungry.

A German officer sat at the far end of the table motioning Burns to help himself to whatever he could find in the way of food on the table. Although the carcass had been picked clean, Jimmy did manage to get a couple of slivers of meat by digging at the bones with his fingers. He spotted a few bread crumbs at one of the place settings, and picked these up by wetting his fingers in his mouth, then pressing them down into the crumbs.

He was licking the crumbs from his fingers when the German officer startled him by saying, in perfect English, "You are with the 299th Engineers, yes?"

Jimmy Burns' face had given him away; he heard the officer say, "One more 299th," and, "Next," as the guard opened the front door and escorted him back out into the cold night.

Jimmy Burns stood there, again shivering for what seemed like hours, as one by one the other prisoners came out of the house after having been interrogated. They were lined up with the usual *"Funf mann"* instructions. By now, it seemed to Burns, the total number of prisoners must be over one hundred.

It suddenly occurred to Jimmy Burns that for the first time since capture, they were outdoors at night, the ideal time to escape. The best time to try to escape, he had been told in lectures, was *as early as possible after capture and preferably at night.* The farther back a prisoner is taken from the front lines, the better organized is the enemy to deal with prisoners. Infantry units are prepared to handle only a few prisoners while engaged in battle; immediately they turn them over to intelligence units for interrogation. When large numbers are captured in battle, it becomes a problem, unless the prisoners can be quickly moved to rear areas, where manpower is available to provide a sufficient number of guards.

Once again, but only by coincidence, Jimmy Burns found himself standing right next to Corporal Jim Kelsey. Quietly, Jimmy Burns asked Kelsey if he had thought about escaping.

Kelsey stuttered from being so cold, and replied, "Yes, but let's wait until we get warm first."

A helpless feeling came over Jimmy Burns as he stood there shivering, wondering what was going to happen to him.

Chapter VII

THE MARCH

Having already been formed up in *funf mann* rows, the prisoners were counted, told to right turn, and to follow the lead guard down the farmhouse driveway. Jimmy Burns was so cold he stumbled along with the rest, hardly realizing that they quickly left the farm property and turned out onto the main road.

The pace was brisk, but everything seemed quiet around him, the snow muffling any sounds of footsteps. The distant noise of battle broke the silence every once in a while. Even though it was a snowy night, the sky lit up from the muzzle blasts of nearby guns.

The column had moved along the road only a short distance when it came to a brief halt. The column started up, only to be halted again after another short distance. This start and stop process was repeated several times.

Jimmy Burns finally realized that part of the group had been separated at each stop, and now his group was being directed off the road into a barnyard. They were now following a guard with a lantern to the rear of a barn. They proceeded through the entrance to a hay barn where they were told to find a place to sleep in the loose hay on the floor.

The guards closed the barn door and stood outside jabbering to each other in German. Right then and there,

Jimmy Burns and Jim Kelsey made a pact to stick together until they could somehow get out of this mess.

"Think we could escape tonight?" asked Jimmy Burns.

"There's only one door, and the guards will be watching it," replied Jim Kelsey. "Besides, I'm too tired. Let's get some sleep first."

Jimmy Burns started to suggest they try hiding in the hay in the morning, but Kelsey was already sound asleep.

The next morning at daylight, the barn door opened, and a German guard moved around the barn poking a rifle butt at lumps in the hay, at the same time shouting, *"Heraus, heraus, schnell, schnell."*

This expression, the prisoners soon learned, meant, "Out, out, quickly, quickly."

Once outside, the prisoners were surprised to see that they were finally going to be fed. A very thick porridge-like soup was being dished out by a couple of farm women. It was a clear, cold morning, and the hot soup was slurped down rapidly by the half-starved prisoners.

Both Kelsey and Burns had kept their canteen belts on throughout the ordeal, so they were lucky to have GI mess cups, even though they did not have spoons with which to eat the soup. Others, not so fortunate, had to use battered old tin cups provided by the farm women.

None of these prisoners had eaten much, except whatever rations they had stuffed into their pockets a couple of days ago. One prisoner approached a guard, and after some discussion, removed his wrist watch, and gave it to the guard in return for a second helping of porridge.

Another gave the guard his gold wedding band, and received a piece of bread, along with a piece of cheese the guard sliced from his own rations.

This scene would prove to be the first of many such degrading acts that Jimmy Burns would witness by hungry prisoners during the next few weeks.

After being allowed to rinse out their cups in cold water,

they filled their canteens with water, using a ladle provided by the guards.

They were marched out to the road where they met other prisoners, formed up again into a long column, walked into another town, and on out the other side. Burns and Kelsey fell into line, both realizing that they had missed their best chance to escape last night. As they walked along, Jimmy Burns kept glancing back, looking at the length of the column he was now a part of. The column stretched on endlessly, and the road constantly curved left, then right, uphill, downhill, so that he could seldom see the front and back at the same time. Jimmy Burns guessed that there might be as many as two hundred prisoners in this line of march.

They stopped to rest about every hour, at which time they would relieve themselves, take a sip of water from their canteens, or scoop up a handful of snow to quench their thirst.

A German officer was at the head of the column; next to him was a German sergeant who relayed the officer's commands to the other guards walking alongside and to the rear of the prisoners. The number of guards seemed small compared to the number of prisoners, but one always showed up as soon as a prisoner dropped out of line to relieve himself along the road. If it happened near a wooded area, the guard would prod the prisoner with his rifle butt, shouting, *"Heraus, heraus."* All efforts to relieve themselves had to be done in the open fields.

A few prisoners tried to escape by dashing into the woods, and wound up with bullets being sprayed at their feet. Several received leg wounds which had to be attended to by medics who had been captured along with other prisoners. Burns and Kelsey repeatedly talked about the fact that the only real chance for escape had eluded them back at the farmhouse the night that they were interrogated.

Toward the end of the first day's march, Jimmy Burns

recognized the town of Wiltz as they passed through it, but after that he was hopelessly lost. He remembered Wiltz from having been there once before on a road sign posting assignment when they were being moved back into Belgium in October. Also, he had talked about this town with the 28th Division lieutenant who had showed up that night at their bridge just before they blew it up. The lieutenant had told him that the 28th Division hospital had been captured intact. Sure enough, there it was, setting on top of a hill, just as they entered the center of the town. The hospital was, actually, a group of large tents with a big sign at the entrance still proclaiming to be *28th Division Field Hospital.*

It was cloudy and snowing, but Jimmy could see plenty of activity going on within the tents, which were torn and ragged looking. American ambulances were lined up in the street loaded with wounded—both German and American—for transport to better facilities, probably back into Germany. Some of the more severely wounded prisoners in the line of march were dropped off here, as the column moved quietly through town.

The routine of separating into small groups and sleeping in hay barns was repeated each night. Sometimes the prisoners received soup at night and coffee in the morning. Other times it would be just soup, always provided by civilians who appeared to be too frightened to speak.

The prisoner column was often halted and moved to the side of the road to let German troops and vehicles pass in the opposite direction. They were replacements on their way up to the battle that was still raging. Each time this happened, Jimmy Burns thought about escaping, but decided that the war could not possibly last much longer.

The German replacements looked like a sorry lot, and the vehicles that passed did not appear to be in very good shape either. The tanks looked okay, but horses were being used to pull artillery pieces, and trucks were pulling each other due to a lack of fuel.

At one such stop, Jimmy saw trucks with German soldiers fanning charcoal fire boxes located on the running boards of trucks. He thought the soldiers were cooking food or simply keeping warm. In fact, these charcoal burning vehicles operated on gas fumes generated by the charcoal burner. A very ingenious vehicle developed by the Germans, but quite slow moving, and not very practical.

Small town after small town was passed through by the column of prisoners that now appeared to number well over three hundred men. New prisoners were being added at each of the overnight stops. The German officer could be seen consulting a map at each rest stop. He was keeping to the back roads and only passing through the smallest of towns.

Although the march was averaging 32 kilometers (20 miles) each day, progression eastward into Germany took several days because of the twisting, turning route. At some point, the march crossed the Our River, a natural boundary separating Luxembourg and Germany. No longer were the sign posts bilingual; heavy German script prevailed and all crossroad signs indicated distances to Bitburg, Trier, Wittlich, Aachen, Bonn, Cologne, Coblenz, and Frankfurt. By subtracting the distances to these major cities, the prisoners were able to estimate how far they had traveled each day.

Some of the guards spoke English and were friendly enough to converse with the prisoners as they walked alongside the column. These guards advised that although the officer had hoped to travel 48 kilometers (30 miles) each day, the march was averaging only about 32 kilometers (20 miles), due to the sick and weakened condition of the prisoners.

Dysentery had become quite prevalent among the prisoners, due to the poor personal hygiene the prisoners were forced to practice. They were eating whatever they could scrounge in the way of food. If a rest stop happened to occur near a field that had yielded food crops the past season, the prisoners would kick their feet into the snow while relieving themselves, searching for an unharvested vegetable in the frozen ground; they would then dig up and eat whatever it was.

At other stops, orchards or sometimes a lone apple tree might be in sight. These trees always had a few small frozen apples hanging from their lower limbs. Prisoners ate these frozen apples, which produced severe stomach cramps, along with the dysentery. Many were so sick they needed help to walk, and some had to be carried on makeshift litters by the other prisoners.

One prisoner who needed help was First Sergeant Flowers of B Company, who had been captured with Jimmy Burns' group. Sergeant Flowers turned out to be one of the biggest sissies in the line of march, just as his name had always implied.

When a prisoner had to be carried, it was up to the members of his own organization to look after him. Otherwise, he would be left to die after being shot by a German guard. This rule had been explained to the prisoners on the very first day of the march. How real this threat was or how many had been killed, Jimmy Burns did not know.

Even though none of the men of B Company had a great fondness for Sergeant Flowers, they all pitched in and took turns carrying him. At first, they carried him on a litter made up of two poles, each of which had been rolled up tightly onto the sides of a GI blanket, with the center section left open for the sergeant to lie on. Where the poles came from, or the blankets for that matter, Jimmy Burns did not know.

After a couple of days using the homemade litter, the men found a real medical stretcher through a bizarre set of circumstances. The column had just started moving again after the second or third rest stop of the morning on a cold, but bright and sunny day. Suddenly, American fighter planes swooped in low, strafing the column of prisoners, scattering them into the fields and ditches alongside the road. Some of the prisoners near the rear of the line were next to a wooded area, which caused great concern among the German guards.

Although the planes made several passes, only a few prisoners were wounded, and fortunately, no one was killed. The wounds were severe, however, and it took a long time to attend to the wounded, as well as to round up all the missing prisoners.

The German officer took this opportunity to move up and down the line of prisoners, delivering an outraged speech in broken English about the "lousy Americans, shooting their own men," etc., etc.

Before moving on, the litter that had been used to carry Sergeant Flowers had to be given up for use by the more seriously wounded prisoners. They now had to carry the sergeant by draping his arms around two men's shoulders and dragging him along as best they could.

The march proceeded up a long hill, where just over the crest, Jimmy Burns saw what the planes were really shooting at. A long convoy of German ambulances sat there, most of them on fire as a result of the attack. Apparently, the prisoner column had simply been in the line of fire, the convoy being the primary target.

Again the German officer flew into a rage, shouting, "Dirty Americans...Roosevelt is a gangster...only savages would shoot at vehicles carrying the Red Cross."

The ambulance drivers could be seen huddled together, close to a barn near the edge of some woods. The planes had departed long ago. Many of the ambulances were burning. Still these drivers made no attempt to put out the fires or to salvage any of the remaining ambulances. Those ambulances not on fire had perfectly good stretchers attached to the side of them by straps.

Soon many prisoners were dashing out of line, returning

with scorched, but usable, litters. Burns and Kelsey transferred Sergeant Flowers to one of these stretchers almost on the run, as the guards were hurrying everyone to get on with the march.

The last of the prisoners had barely passed the row of ambulances when a fireworks display erupted, such as Jimmy Burns had never seen in his life. Ammunition was exploding and shooting through the air, coming from the burning ambulances. The American planes had somehow correctly guessed that this convoy bearing the Red Cross symbol was a disguised ammunition supply fleet. The eruption was dangerous and dispersed the prisoners again. Originally angered by the attack, they now felt gratified that the Germans had been unsuccessful with their little game of deception.

Sergeant Flowers moaned and groaned, begged for water or food, and overall, became a pain in the neck. Carrying the litter was exhausting, but they all took turns for about eight days, after which he was left off at a hospital in Limburg, Germany.

Before reaching Limburg, however, there was more hardship on the prisoners, including Burns and Kelsey. The column had stopped for a rest. Kelsey was returning from a trip into a field, with a puny little frozen apple in his grasp. The group had started to move when Kelsey, hurrying to rejoin Burns in the line of march, fell over a large snowbank into the ditch alongside the road. Kelsey was exhausted, and was trying to regain his feet, when a guard prodded him with his rifle butt. Kelsey was almost on his feet, but fell again, because the guard pushed the rifle butt hard into his backside.

Jimmy Burns slipped out of his position in line and rushed back to help Kelsey. The guard then jabbed the rifle butt at Burns, aiming at his arms, but striking a blow that glanced off Jimmy Burns' shoulder and struck him on the side of the face. Jimmy Burns saw stars and struck back at the guard with his fists. He hurt his hand on the guard's rifle, and was then butted several more times in the rear as he helped Kelsey back into the line. Kelsey was struck several more times, as well, during the process. They both staggered back up to their position, as the guard followed, shouting at them incessantly.

The column of prisoners crossed the Rhine River somewhere in the vicinity of Coblenz. They did not enter this large city, but crossed over a small bridge south of it, after wandering for hours along the banks of the huge river. After crossing the river, the route followed a narrow road that slowly climbed to higher elevation. A winter storm slowed the progress of the prisoner column for two days. Snow squalls and icy winds beat against their faces, producing frozen beards on the men. Heel blisters were rubbed raw by wet boots. Weariness and hunger caused many to fall out of the column before the group finally reached Limburg.

Here the prisoners received the worst blow of all when they were put up overnight in padded cells. The building that they were locked up in was located on the grounds of a large hospital in the center of the city. This building had housed insane people at one time. The rooms were arranged in cell blocks as one would expect to see in any prison, except that each was completely padded. There was only a small opening, high up on the entrance wall, through which air could enter or leave.

So many prisoners were crowded into one tiny cell that the air became hot, stuffy, stinky, and sickening. The prisoners were let out once during the night to relieve themselves. In the morning they were let out again, fed some hot broth, then returned to the padded cells for what seemed an eternity. Actually, only a total of twenty-four hours elapsed, but great anxiety existed among the prisoners. Each of them thought he was going to be permanently confined in a padded cell. Many of the prisoners became nauseated. Vomiting occurred, which had to be collected in their helmet liners for later disposal. When they were finally released from the cells, most of them were in worse shape than when they had entered the day before.

Upon leaving the hospital grounds, the prisoners saw further evidence of indiscriminate bombing and strafing by American planes. The German guards were quick to point out a warehouse-type building, completely flattened by a bombing raid the previous night. None of the prisoners recalled hearing the bombing, probably because they were in padded cells. The roof of the building was still intact, lying on the rubble beneath it with huge Red Cross panels stretched across the roof. The panels looked new, and appeared to have been placed there temporarily.

Whether the hospital or some of its buildings contained military supplies, the prisoners did not know. They had seen previous evidence of the Germans hiding ammunition in ambulances, so were suspicious of this incident.

They were relieved to leave this place, but also anxious to learn what awaited them next. Limburg had been mentioned as the final destination early in the march.

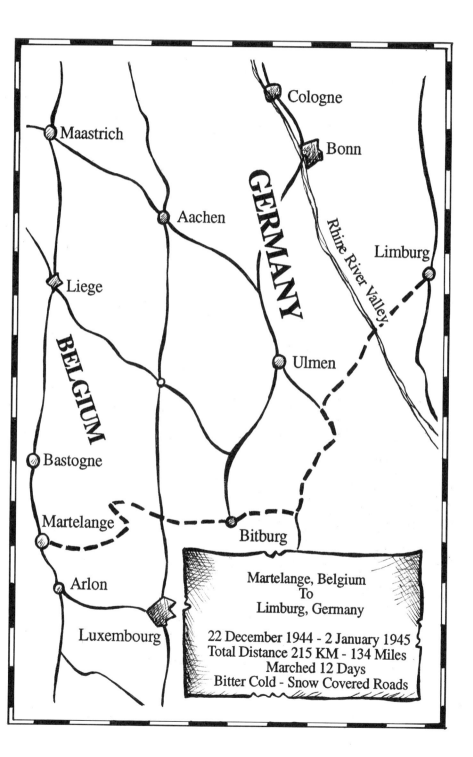

Maastrich

Cologne

Bonn

GERMANY

Aachen

Rhine River Valley

Limburg

Liege

BELGIUM

Ulmen

Bastogne

Martelange

Bitburg

Arlon

Luxembourg

Martelange, Belgium
To
Limburg, Germany

22 December 1944 - 2 January 1945
Total Distance 215 KM - 134 Miles
Marched 12 Days
Bitter Cold - Snow Covered Roads

Chapter VIII

STALAG

It was only a short walk from the hospital to the outskirts of the city, where the prisoners saw for the first time in their lives a prisoner of war camp: Stalag 12A. The road leading to the camp descended gradually along a ridge that overlooked a wide valley. As they walked down this road, the prisoners could see barbed wire fences enclosing the camp. At the bottom of the hill, the column turned left off the main road, then up a slight grade to the camp entrance. It looked to Jimmy Burns as if the camp had been built in a large gravel pit, with only the entrance available from flat ground.

"How clever," he thought, "to use natural terrain as a barrier to escape."

Even if one could get over the fences, a steep bank surrounded the camp on three sides. The prisoners were marched through the front gates, split off into groups, and assigned to barracks.

Jimmy Burns and Kelsey selected a double bunk together. They were deciding who would get the top or bottom bunk when a tall American walked into the room, announcing that he was the camp commander. He said his name was Corporal Grey and that he was in charge, because when he had entered this camp—some months ago—none of the other non-commissioned officers captured with him had been man enough to take on the job. Corporal Grey was a real smooth talker. He attempted to win the new prisoners' support by congratulating them on their appearance as they had marched into the camp. He said that he knew immediately they were all non-commissioned officers by the way they carried themselves, walking erect and in cadence, as they had been trained to do.

The prisoners all glanced at one another with a quizzical look because, personally, they all knew that they looked like hell.

Corporal Grey explained the camp rules, how the committees worked, and the processing procedure that was to take place at this camp.

The first order of business was to get everyone registered as an official prisoner of war. So far, the German guards had only been counting prisoners, not recording names, rank, units, next of kin, etc. Somewhere, back at the battle, the American Army had presumably listed them all as *Missing in Action*. Each prisoner filled out a personal data card which was to be turned into the German *kommandant's* office by the committee members. It took a long time to complete this task due to a shortage of pencils.

The prisoners were then each given a blanket and a mattress cover made of gunny sack material. They were then directed to a pile of straw at one end of the camp, where the covers could be filled with straw.

Each barrack had bunks for about fifty men. The one that Burns and Kelsey occupied was completely filled with prisoners. Climbing into the upper bunk required careful balance because the bunks were old and wobbly. A small stove stood at the far end of the room, but neither coal nor wood was available for it. A corner room in each barrack served as a supply room; a second room provided sleeping quarters for the American commander's committee members. The committee members had been prisoners for some time and looked quite healthy, as well as clean.

After receiving soup and a piece of bread each, Jimmy Burns and Jim Kelsey turned in to sleep on a mattress for the first time in weeks.

Before falling to sleep, the two engaged in their usual conversation regarding escape. They were quite elated to hear that day that they were encouraged to try to escape, but should first report their plans to the American camp commander's escape committee. They were promised that the committee would help and furnish the best advice available to aid in their escape. They were also warned that without the committee's help an attempt to escape would be practically useless. How could they possibly expect to find their way back to the American lines now? Over a period of ten or twelve days they had marched about 215 kilometers, almost 135 miles. And who knew where the American lines were at this time? The German drive was rolling pretty good when it blew past them in Martelange. The problem was mind boggling.

A prisoner identifying himself as Ed Horton rose up from his bunk across the aisle and walked over to talk to Burns and Kelsey.

"I've been listening to you guys talk about escape, and I have some advice for you. Don't try it. I've just returned from thirty days in a padded cell at the Limburg Hospital because I got caught trying to escape. My friend Johnny Riordan got shot in the hip by a guard and may still be in the hospital. Maybe he's dead, I really don't know."

He glanced over his shoulder, then whispered, "This escape committee is in cahoots with the Germans. They gave us a map showing how to get to the railroad yards, but when we got there the place was crawling with Germans. I gave up, but Johnny tried to make a run for it. I'm sure someone on the committee must have tipped them off. When I asked them about it I was transferred down here with you new prisoners. My hunch is there's going to be a shipment of prisoners out of here real soon. Take my advice and wait awhile."

"Why would the committee help you escape, then turn you in?" asked Jim Kelsey.

"Take a close look at some of these committee guys. They don't look like they're starving, do they?" replied Ed Horton.

"Geez! I thought we were all going to get some decent food here." said Jimmy Burns.

"No, the food and everything else around here is terrible unless you are in the committee click."

These were Ed Horton's final words as he returned to his bunk and turned in.

Getting to sleep was tough enough without this new worry to think about. Was Ed Horton telling the truth? Would Americans really turn against their own countrymen to get a better deal for themselves? Jimmy Burns couldn't believe a soldier would do this. This idea was against all principles of camaraderie that he had observed since being in the Army.

In addition to these worries, there was the problem of being cold. The building was poorly constructed and drafty. Several broken windows were covered with cardboard. Wind whistled through the cracks and around the window frames. The little stove would have helped, but there was no fire in it. Even though he slept with all his clothes on, one blanket was not enough to keep Jimmy Burns warm. He had removed his wet boots from his feet, which were numb from the cold and ached constantly. He could see steam vapor from his breath as he stared up at the dimly lit ceiling overhead. The mattress smelled from previous use. The straw pricked his body right through his clothing. He scratched his head and groin because lice had infested both areas. It was almost impossible to sleep.

The next morning after receiving hot coffee for breakfast, the prisoners were marched to an administration building located in another compound. Here they were interviewed, one at a time, by a group of Americans with German officers overseeing the operation. Each man was given a small pouch and told to put all his valuables into it for return to his next of kin. The American sergeant who interviewed Jimmy Burns advised him not to hold anything back because the Germans would only confiscate it later.

Into the pouch went money, rings, watches, and GI dog tags. Jimmy Burns was issued a new brass tag with a prisoner of war number stamped on it. His new number was 095123. Finger prints and other bits of vital information were added to the personal data cards filled out the day before. Jimmy Burns and Jim Kelsey followed the American sergeant's orders explicitly. Later they learned from Ed Horton that the Americans processing them were a bunch of crooks and kept all those personal items for themselves, probably sharing them with the Germans.

Upon returning to his assigned barrack, Jimmy Burns noticed that many of those captured with him were now missing. Only non-commissioned officers were now present in the barrack, i.e., corporal or higher in rank. There was Staff Sergeant Hogar, Sergeant Coon, Sergeant Rod, Sergeant Durr, Corporals Jimmy Burns and Jim Kelsey.

Frenchie was there. Being a gunner he held the rank of technical corporal. All the privates and privates first class captured with them had been sent off to work camps. According to Geneva Convention rules for prisoners of war, non-commissioned officers were not required to work, except voluntarily, and then only in the supervisory capacity.

Some of the other so called noncoms in the barrack had bragged to Jimmy Burns that they were really privates, but had bribed the Americans processing them to change their records. Had he only known this was possible, Jimmy Burns could have kept Frank, Fred, Francis, Wiltsy, Andy and the others together with the rest of the group. For one pack of cigarettes a prisoner could become a corporal; for two packs, a sergeant. The price went up, the higher the rank one wanted to be assigned.

Neither Burns nor Kelsey had any cigarettes, but they could have found them among the sergeants, some of whom they knew did not smoke. Sergeants Hogar and Durr were known to hoard cigarettes, then sell them to others at a profit. This had been going on since basic training, and Jimmy Burns had seen each of them bartering with cigarettes for food along the line of march.

Ever since capture, conversation among the prisoners had been limited to "Where are we?" "Where are we going?" "When will we get there?" or topics relating to the battle.

Although the prisoners tended to march alongside people they knew, the position in the line of march was not regulated. Jimmy Burns and Jim Kelsey stayed together, but often found themselves among prisoners they did not know.

They learned that the battle was widespread, but never did gain a clear picture of how it had all happened. Everyone seemed to have an interesting story about his own capture.

Now at Stalag 12A, the new prisoners were learning all about prison camp life from those that been imprisoned much earlier in the war. A prisoner of war camp was supposed to be safe and comfortable for its occupants. The enemy was bound by the Geneva Convention to keep prisoners safely confined away from battle areas. Furthermore, they were to provide adequate food, clothing, and shelter, at least equal to that provided to their own troops. Recreation was to be made available, as well as books and mail from home to help pass the time in confinement. The International Red Cross was to inspect camps periodically to see that these rules were complied with. The Red Cross could also supplement rations with food parcels. All this Jimmy Burns learned in the first few days at Stalag 12A.

This camp failed to meet the requirements of the Geneva Convention on all counts. It was neither safe nor comfortable. Every day American bombers attacked the railroad yard which was only a mile or two from the camp.

Going to the bathroom was the most uncomfortable routine of the day. Toilets were little more than large outhouses with some kind of septic system that didn't work. Raw sewage flowed out of the ground near a pile of lime that was spread over the leakage. Lime was also poured into the toilet pits to disinfect them. The floor of the toilet building was slippery from urine that never quite made it into the crapper because prisoners couldn't wait for a seat to open up.

The only place to wash was at an outdoor trough where only the cold water line emitted a trickle to keep it from freezing. Neither soap nor towels were available. Prisoners rinsed their hands and spread water on their hairy faces, then ran inside to wipe dry on their blankets or clothing.

The food didn't even come close to meeting the requirements that it be equal to that provided to their own troops. If the German army had to subsist on what was fed to the prisoners, the war would not have lasted very long. The coffee tasted like weak tea and was called *ersatz* which meant it was made from something other than the coffee bean; just what it was made from, remained a mystery. The soup was revolting and looked like hot greasy dishwater. Purported to be a vegetable beef soup, any meat used as a base had been removed from the pots before being delivered to the prisoners. There were chunks of vegetables, either kohlrabi or rutabaga, both of which looked and tasted like turnip. The only way the prisoners could distinguish one from the other was by the color: the kohlrabi was white, and rutabaga, yellowish.

Bread was delivered by the Germans to the committee room sometime during the day with an announcement of how many men had to share a loaf. Sometimes it would be six or seven men to a loaf; most of the time it would be five. The repeated promise of Red Cross parcels was never fulfilled. The only thing that kept Jimmy Burns going was the thought that the war could not last much longer.

All indications seemed to point toward staying at Stalag 12A for the rest of the war. The committee in his barrack urged everyone to sign up for books to read. Other options would be French or German lessons, crafts, recreational sports, and discussion groups.

Jimmy Burns started German lessons with a committee member who had been a high school teacher prior to military service. Since no one else signed up for this class, Jimmy had a private tutor for about seven days of lessons. He quickly learned that stalag was an abbreviation for *stammlager* meaning main camp. The Germans assigned numbers and letters to each stalag, which had something to do with the regional location of each camp.

Fortunately, the stay at this camp would prove to be a short one. More and more American prisoners kept pouring in, and one day a group of about three hundred prisoners was called out, lined up in *funf mann* columns and marched to the railroad yards in Limburg. Jimmy Burns and his friends were included in this contingent.

It was learned that an American master sergeant named Adams was in charge as American commander. This man had been at the head of the column all along the march and was in charge of this group right from the beginning. Sergeant Adams had attempted to assume command of the American compound, which was his rightful duty as senior non-commissioned officer. This caused a problem with Corporal Grey, who was a big phoney, but had the German camp *kommandant* in his hip pocket. A large group had to be shipped out of the camp, so the German *kommandant* seized the opportunity to remove Sergeant Adams and most of his followers.

It was cold and raining as they marched out of the camp past the railway station, to a siding far down the tracks. Burns and Kelsey hoped the direction of the train would be favorable for escape. Ed Horton had left the barracks with them and had promised to include them in his escape plans. They never saw him again.

Jimmy Burns felt that he had to make an escape attempt to impress his Uncle Tip that he was tough enough to continue a career as a regular Army soldier. Why was it so important to impress his Uncle Tip? He didn't know the answer to this question. He also felt an obligation to Sergeant Eddie Boyd, but knew that Eddie would approve of whatever action he took.

Stalag 12A - Limburg

Chapter IX

TRAIN RIDE

The long line of prisoners had halted between two rows of boxcars well beyond the Limburg train station.

"The Germans must be ashamed of our appearance," Jimmy thought. "They are hiding us from view of the civilian passengers in the station."

He was not aware that there were no civilian passengers in the train station. Only military trains dared to operate in this region of Germany, and then only under the cover of darkness. When the weather was clear, Allied planes repeatedly attacked trains and stations, making travel by train during daylight hours virtually impossible.

The Limburg railway station looked more like a freight depot than a passenger station to Jimmy Burns. The window frames had bars on them, reminding him of the old Delaware, Lackawanna and Western freight depot in his home town. When he was a youngster, Jimmy Burns' family had lived near a railroad crossing, not too far from the DL&W depot. He watched many trains pass by his house, and could easily identify the various types of freight cars that moved slowly past the crossing daily.

Standing in the railroad yard at Limburg, he realized that these boxcars did not look like any that he had ever seen before. The cars were smaller and seemed to be setting higher above the track than he remembered. There were narrow spaces between the horizontal boards of the cars, suggesting that the cars might be used to transport animals. On the other hand, each car had a set of steps attached to the door opening which would seem to indicate that only people were placed in them. Apparently, the cars were used for both purposes.

Jimmy Burns still thought the prisoners were going to be marched back to the train station to board a conventional passenger train.

The German guards opened the car doors, one at a time, and directed the prisoners to enter. As he climbed into the car immediately in front of his group, Jimmy Burns observed a thin layer of straw on the floor and a metal plate in the center of the car where a stove had once stood. There was a small open window high up in one of the walls with a hinged cover that could be closed. The German guards counted the prisoners and closed the door when the number of men in a car reached fifty. It soon became apparent that this was twice as many people as the car could hold comfortably.

The first prisoners to enter sat down along the walls and stretched their legs out in front of them to relax. As more and more prisoners came into the car it became obvious that there was not enough room for everyone to sit in that position. Burns and Kelsey quickly located a place to sit in one corner of the car. They pulled their knees into their chests allowing others to stand, sit or kneel in the area between themselves and prisoners on the opposite wall. A constant grumbling was heard from those prisoners still standing or kneeling. Finally someone took charge of the situation and spoke up loudly to announce that cooperation was necessary to get everyone seated in a comfortable position. This man moved about the car putting everyone in the sit-squat position that Burns and Kelsey had already assumed. This arrangement provided sitting space for all but one of the prisoners: the man that directed everyone to sit the way he had suggested.

It was decided the one standing position would be located near the window and rotated hourly. This allowed the prisoners to keep a watch on what was happening outside the car. Everyone was anxious to get a look at the outside and welcomed the opportunity to stand up occasionally. A pair of binoculars was produced which were kept in the hands of the observer at all times.

The prisoner sitting next to Jimmy Burns was a tall lanky man with thick glasses and a distinct German accent. His name was Fred Koeningsberger, which he had changed to Fred King during processing at Stalag 12A. He explained to Jimmy Burns that he had been born in Germany, but because his parents were Jewish the family had fled to the United States in 1936. It would not go well for Fred if the Germans were to learn about his background. Fred suggested that he should be at the window when the train moved because he could read German signs and had traveled throughout Germany with his parents. This suggestion was passed to the man at the window, with the simple explanation that Fred could read German signs. The train did not move for several hours so Jimmy Burns learned a good deal about pre-war Germany from Fred King.

Fred explained that although his family lived on the eastern border of Germany, his father operated an import-export business, and the family traveled extensively in Europe. Fred talked about how Hitler had risen to power because most Germans were poor and hungry, waiting for someone like Hitler to lead them out of their unhappy situation. Germany's problems developed as a result of the World War I Armistice. Germany had to give up land to France, Poland, Hungary and Czechoslovakia. Furthermore, the required payments in cash to the allies had completely exhausted the Germany treasury.

Prior to the 1936 Olympics, held in Berlin that year,

there was very little food available in Germany. Such staples as milk, bread, eggs, and butter were difficult to find, and sold at very high prices on the black market. Likewise, travel by automobile was almost impossible due to a shortage of fuel. Public transportation was crowded, even though it could only be afforded by the very rich. Nevertheless, Fred had traveled with his father to Berlin in 1936 to witness the Olympics. He spoke of the utter amazement with which he and his father viewed the plentiful food and goods available in Berlin that year. Restaurants served excellent meals, and markets displayed all the foods that had been non-existent in the past. Even the department stores had ample inventories of clothing and household goods for sale. Fred explained that this seemingly abundance of supply was really a propaganda move. After the Olympics were completed, the situation returned to one of shortages once again. The whole affair had been arranged to convince the rest of the world that Hitler had turned the German economy around, and to hide the fact that Germany was preparing for war.

The seating arrangement worked out satisfactorily for a short period of time. It soon became evident that the prisoners had to stand up anyway to relieve leg cramps and stiff back muscles. Furthermore, they had to relieve themselves by using a steel helmet and passing it to the window observer for disposal. The odor in the car was bad enough when the prisoners had first entered; it was quickly becoming unbearable. Jimmy Burns was shocked to learn that instead of animal odors, the straw on the floor reeked of human urine and excrement. Now the fresh smell of piss and crap caused many of the prisoners to vomit, which only added to the foul environment.

The train sat there on a siding until darkness settled in. A sharp jolt gave signal to the fact that an engine had coupled up to the train of boxcars. The train moved slowly down the track, past the station, leaving Stalag 12A behind, as only one of many stops on a journey of hardship for the prisoners.

Fred King took his turn at the window long enough to determine that the train was heading south toward Frankfurt. That night both Kelsey and Burns had a turn at the window. Each reported deepening snow depths on the ground and a clear moonlit night.

The train ride was cold, the only warmth coming from the body heat generated by the prisoners in the car. The men gradually became accustomed to the foul air, but the slop bucket continued to be used throughout the night. It was almost dawn when the train stopped, again on a siding, amid rows and rows of seemingly empty boxcars. The car doors were opened, and the prisoners were allowed to get out to relieve themselves.

They were then marched to the rear car of the train where they received coffee and a small piece of bread. The German guards occupied the last car, which was a conventional passenger coach with the rear third converted to a kitchen facility.

After being returned to the boxcars, the prisoners quickly settled into the seating assignment of the previous day. The men assumed the train would be moving on, but a series of start-stop-reverse actions resulted in the cars being located once again on a remote siding. Fred King was posted at the window throughout this maneuvering and was able to report that the train was in the Frankfurt railroad complex, a long way from the main station.

A strange silence settled in as the prisoners dozed or listened for some indication of what was going to happen next.

About noon that day the silence was broken by the sound of Allied planes bombing and strafing the railroad station. The planes made several passes at the terminal. The raid lasted well over an hour. As soon as the noise of bombing subsided, it would be followed by the sound of low flying planes strafing the same area again and again. Another period of silence was followed by the sound of a high speed train moving rapidly through the railroad complex. The military trains stopped short of the cities during bombing periods, the personnel aboard scattering into the woods until the *all clear* signal was sounded. The train would then race on to its destination unless stopped by another attack at some other rail city along the route.

The prisoner train remained stationary in the quiet confines of empty boxcars at the Frankfurt yards.

Finally, the rattle and squeak of the boxcars could be heard, and the prisoner train started moving, again heading south through many small towns. Fred King called out the names of the towns and predicted the train must be heading in the direction of Bavaria, the southernmost section of Germany.

When Fred returned from his position at the window, he explained that the chances of escaping would diminish as the train proceeded further south. Bavaria was mountainous and wooded, which would provide good cover, but snow depths would make travel difficult.

Although the train was moving south, it was also carrying them easterly away from France, which would be the best location to head for. Eventually, Switzerland would be closer; however, the borders to this country were well guarded even before the war. Also the terrain became even more rugged in the direction of Switzerland. With each sentence uttered by Fred King, Burns and Kelsey recognized that their plans for escape were hopeless. Still, they talked about it and intended to try if the opportunity presented itself.

After three more nights of travel, with daily stops on sidings but without air raids, Fred announced the train had arrived at Stuttgart.

The process of disembarking each morning, followed by a meal of coffee or soup, became a standard procedure.

Each time they were let out of the boxcars, Burns and Kelsey talked about trying to escape. Upon reaching the ground, they always found that they could hardly walk, let alone run, which would be required to get out of sight quickly.

The Stuttgart rail complex looked completely destroyed. Nevertheless, it was bombed again that day as the prisoner train sat helpless on a siding. German military trains, containing complete army staffs, could be seen moving quickly through the area as soon as the bombing stopped. As usual, the train containing the prisoners departed from Stuttgart much later in the day, under the cover of darkness.

Several more days passed before the prisoner train reached Munich, where the devastation looked to be worse than either Frankfurt or Stuttgart. At each of these major cities the prisoner train was shuttled about the railroad yards for hours before being positioned for the day.

Many nights they waited on remote sidings for long periods until another train passed by on the main track. The train would then proceed slowly for the balance of the night to the next stop. At each stop the prisoners thought surely they would be taken from the train and marched to a stalag. After leaving Munich, the train headed north and seemed to travel much faster, even travelling during daylight hours occasionally.

One day Fred reported that the train was close to Berlin, although passing well to the east of the capital city of Germany. The train stopped that day in Frankfurt, which caused a great deal of confusion among the prisoners in the car occupied by Jimmy Burns.

Fred quickly explained that Germany had two cities with the same name. The one they had passed through several days earlier was called Frankfurt-am-Main; this one was on the Oder River, therefore, was called Frankfurt-an-der-Oder. The Allied planes must have known there were two Frankfurts, because this one was bombed also while the prisoner train sat, once again, helpless on a remote siding.

The last two nights of travel sent the train directly north to a town called Stargard. Fred King noted the location of Stargard as being near a much larger city called Stettin, a border city in Poland prior to German occupation. The train had stopped a great distance past the train station as it usually did at all stations along the route. This time, however, the train remained on the main track even though the doors were not opened for quite some time.

When the doors were finally opened, the prisoners were marched toward the station, turned left onto a service road, then left again at the main highway. The column was now moving away from Stargard in the direction of Stettin, 40 kilometers away. This caused some concern among the prisoners, who were in no condition to walk that distance.

The prisoners had been confined on the old train for fifteen days with very little to eat, hardly any water, and very unsanitary conditions. The strength and spirit of the men had been completely drained. The train ride was so debilitating that not one of the prisoners had attempted to escape. Although everyone was sick, miraculously, no one had died.

Soon the column turned off the main road and proceeded along a side road to the entrance of Stalag 2D. As shabby as this camp looked, it was still a welcome sight to the prisoners who were relieved to be leaving the ugly boxcars for good. They were all very sick and extremely tired from the ordeal of the train ride. Slowly they shuffled and stumbled through the gates of what they assumed would be their final stop for the duration of the war.

After passing through the main gate, the prisoners walked past a building with a sign on it stating that it was the camp *kommandant's* office. They turned left through another set of gates and into a small compound of the huge camp.

Once inside the compound, they were lined up, and a German sergeant started shouting, *"Funf mann, funf mann."*

completed. The prisoners were separated into groups of fifty and assigned to barracks. Burns and Kelsey stayed together as usual, each admitting that the hope for an escape was probably over.

Jimmy Burns decided it was no longer worth worrying what Uncle Tip or Sergeant Eddie Boyd might think of him. Surviving was going to be difficult enough. He had to consider what was best for him regardless of what others might think. An Army career or becoming an officer meant little to him right now.

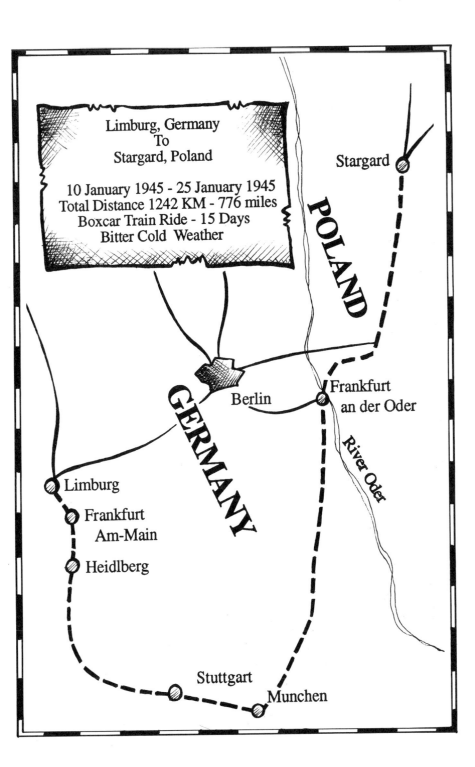

Limburg, Germany
To
Stargard, Poland

10 January 1945 - 25 January 1945
Total Distance 1242 KM - 776 miles
Boxcar Train Ride - 15 Days
Bitter Cold Weather

POLAND

Stargard

GERMANY

Berlin

Frankfurt
an der Oder

River Oder

Limburg

Frankfurt
Am-Main

Heidlberg

Stuttgart

Munchen

Chapter X

STARGARD

Stalag 2D at Stargard was much larger than Stalag 12A, from which the prisoners had been removed for the long train ride. The American compound, however, was quite small, consisting of only six barracks and a latrine. The compound was located close to the main gate in one corner of the huge camp. The barracks were even more spartan than those at Stalag 12A. Each barrack was divided into four large rooms with a center hallway passing through the building lengthwise. A small committee room was located in the front left corner of each building. Burns and Kelsey found that there were no bunks or mattresses to sleep on. Instead, they were advised to select a spot along the wall on which to place their blankets for sleeping.

A cement hearth in one corner of the room gave evidence to a stove having once been located there. The rooms probably had wooden bunks originally, the bunks having been dismantled and burned as firewood long ago. It was a dismal setting that Burns and Kelsey faced as they bedded down that first night at Stalag 2D and tried to sleep. For hours they talked about hunger and the possibility of escape.

When first captured, the Americans had among them several doctors and medical corpsmen but these had all been removed from the group during the trip to Stalag 2D.

Several English prisoners were now assigned to the American compound to look after the medical needs of the American prisoners. These British prisoners were all well trained in first aid and had been in captivity for a long time. These experienced prisoners taught the Americans many little tricks to ease the hardship of imprisonment, including the *buddy* system that Burns and Kelsey had already adopted. There was so little of everything; combining and sharing seemed the natural thing to do. Two blankets covering a pair of prisoners provided greater warmth than one blanket used singly. The British called their system *mucking together*. Each British prisoner referred to his partner as his *mucker*.

Shortly after arriving at Stalag 2D, the Americans were taken to a building on the hospital grounds for the purpose of taking a shower and shaving, for the first time since capture. They took their clothes off in one room and piled them on benches along a wall. The prisoners were shuttled through a door into a large shower room, where they huddled together in groups under a shower head to lather as best they could with a bar of hard brown soap.

Jimmy Burns was astonished to see that his feet were blackened around his toes, along the bottoms, and up his heels almost to the ankle.

"Hey," he shouted to Kelsey, "my feet are turning black."

"So are mine," replied Kelsey, "and they hurt like hell."

Jimmy Burns looked down at the feet of the other prisoners sharing the shower head with Kelsey and him. Sure enough, they all had black or dark blue feet. This was the result of frostbite suffered by all of them during the early days of captivity. Prior to the thawing out of his feet by the hot shower, Jimmy Burns had not had feeling in either of his feet. Now he was suffering an aching feeling that extended up the calves of his legs. The pain was so intense he could hardly walk to move about in the shower area. While rubbing his feet during the shower, gobs of skin sloughed off, and he had no sense of feel in the blackened parts.

When the shower was off, the prisoners took turns with a few safety razors and shaved off stubbly beards. Some preferred not to shave, so began the growth of a beard for the first time in their lives.

As the prisoners returned to the room where they had left their clothes, the smell of cyanide gas was overpowering, causing some of the prisoners to become sick immediately. The clothing had been deloused by this gas; therefore, hundreds of fleas and lice fell to the floor as the prisoners gathered up their clothes to dress.

Jimmy Burns and those other prisoners without overcoats were directed to pick one from a pile on the floor in one corner of the room. The coats were from captured supplies of the French army; hence, they were light blue in color with gray trim on the collars. The coat that Jimmy Burns selected was much too large for him, but it was warm, and he felt much better having this extra protection from the weather.

The American commander had his committees in full operation on the second day of the prisoners' arrival at Stalag 2D. Daily rations of coffee, bread, and soup were distributed. A progress report on the war was read each morning, and the prisoners were constantly reminded not to try an escape without first contacting the escape committee.

At many stalags the American camp commander was affectionately known as the MOC or Man of Confidence. This expression easily translated to *Mac*; thus, the camp commander became Sergeant Mac. Here at Stalag 2D, as a joke, the word *fuhrer* was attached to all titles associated with leaders. The American camp commander was known as camp fuhrer, his assistants as barracks fuhrer. Even a room fuhrer had been appointed for each room. Burns and Kelsey occupied a room in which Fred King (Koeningsberger) had been appointed room fuhrer because of his knowledge of the German language.

After only a few days at Stalag 2D, Burns and Kelsey were convinced that survival under existing conditions would be difficult. Both were running a fever, looked jaundiced, and spent almost twenty-four hours each day huddled in their blankets trying to keep warm. They got up only to eat the paltry rations being served, to stand in line for *appells* or to go to the latrine, the latter happening too frequently to suit either of them. In their weakened condition they paid little attention to the daily war bulletins which were very optimistic about the outcome of the war.

Because Burns and Kelsey had befriended Fred King during the train ride, they were able to extract one great big favor from him. Fred arranged to have the two of them transferred to the first-aid barracks for a few days of better food and medication. The British prisoners had a fair amount of first-aid equipment that had been issued to them by the Germans. The room was clean, heated, and equipped with soft mats on which the ailing prisoners slept. There were extra blankets available, which added even more comfort than either Burns or Kelsey thought was possible.

The British served tea, cookies, beef, crackers, margarine, cheese, and chocolate, as well as dispensing pills daily to Jimmy Burns and Jim Kelsey. The pills were to reduce fever and seemed to work, even though they were only aspirin.

The British prisoners were cheerful and always optimistic about the future outcome of the situation at Stalag 2D. One of their helpers was an American medic named Ralph who emitted confidence, making jokes about every aspect of prison life. After three days, Burns and Kelsey felt strong enough to take a short walk. The two would liked to have stayed longer, but space was limited, and three days was as long as each prisoner was allowed to stay there.

Early the next morning they reported outside for *appell*, then returned to their own barrack room much stronger, ready to plan an escape.

When Jimmy and Kelsey went to the escape committee they did not have a good, workable escape plan, and expected to get turned down. Their purpose, primarily, was to get a look at the committee room and staff, who Burns and Kelsey suspected were living a good deal more comfortably than the rest of the *kriegies*. They had heard many rumors to this effect during their recent stay at the dispensary. While they listened to the escape committee sergeant explain the negatives of trying to escape, the two prisoners noted that there were many blankets, food supplies, cigarettes and even a radio in plain sight. They had not seen any of these items in the previous prisoner of war camp. The sergeant even gave them each a cup of coffee and a cigarette while he talked, finally advising them that at this time all escape attempts were forbidden due to the remote location of the camp.

Just as they were leaving, someone from their own barracks came in and announced that one of the regular ration crew members was too sick to report in the morning to help carry the morning coffee to the barracks. Although Kelsey quickly volunteered, it soon became apparent to them that not everyone was acceptable for this assignment. After a few minutes discussion of alternates, Kelsey was told to show the crew chief where his bunk was, so that he could be awakened early to go with the rest of the crew to the prison kitchen. What a stroke of luck, Jimmy Burns thought. Both he and Kelsey had tried for weeks to get on this crew, because they suspected that the crew received extra rations.

It was actually hard work; two men had to carry a large container that resembled the huge institutional cooking pots used in military kitchens and restaurants. A pot contained twenty-five or thirty gallons of coffee and weighed more than two healthy men would choose to carry; much less would it be the choice of underweight and emaciated prisoners. The prison kitchen was a half mile away. Carrying coffee was not the kind of job one volunteered for unless there was a worthwhile reason for doing so. This task was performed each morning and again in the evening. In the evening the container was filled with soup instead of coffee.

The morning following the talk with the escape committee, Kelsey was awakened early and went with the ration crew to the prison kitchen. While he was waiting in line with a partner to have their pot filled with coffee, he noticed one of the commander's staff holding a smaller pot that he was apparently going to carry all alone. Kelsey suspected this container was special and offered to help carry it. When he reached out for it with his free hand he was rebuked by the staff member who pulled it forcibly from Kelsey's grasp, knocking the cover off. A quick peek inside assured Kelsey that it contained not coffee, but bread, margarine, jam, and even sausage. This explained why the commander's staff was so fussy about who they let participate in this ration crew business. The staff member carried this relatively lightweight pot all alone; a couple of other staff members carried a similar pot containing coffee to the commander's room.

Kelsey and the other ration crew members each were given a heel of bread as a reward for their efforts and advised to keep their mouths shut about what they had seen that morning. Try as he may, Kelsey could never get this assignment again. It was apparent why the staff people looked healthy and seemed to be more contented with captivity than the rest of the prisoners.

A few days after Kelsey's stint on the ration crew, a short, chubby blonde prisoner walked into their barracks and announced he was a chaplain's assistant looking for a Catholic with altar boy experience. Jimmy Burns was selected to help with mass to be celebrated in the French compound on Sunday. He was told to be ready about eight o'clock the following Sunday to go with Whitey, as they all called him. The other prisoners were advised they could attend the mass but could not leave until almost nine o'clock, the time at which mass was scheduled. Jimmy cleaned himself as best he could, shaved with a sharp GI knife, wiped the mud off his boots, and met Whitey promptly at eight o'clock the following Sunday.

Whitey had two other men with him and carried a small tote bag which Jimmy assumed must contain the priest's accessories. The four prisoners were let through a gate and walked unescorted past the building housing the German *kommandant's* office. The group turned left at the camp kitchen, through another set of gates, and up a lane separating two compounds, with barbed wire on either side of the lane. Prisoners were clustered near each compound fence. Those on the left appeared to be Russian. Prisoners on the right were shouting to them in French. During the walk up the lane, Whitey advised that only one altar boy was required, but by bribing the German guards he was able to get two or three helpers into the French compound early. One would serve as altar boy, while the others moved freely about the French compound bartering for food with cigarettes that Whitey had been able to scrounge from other prisoners. The tote bag he was carrying contained cigarettes and chocolate.

Entrance to the French compound was gained at the end of the lane, and the prisoners proceeded to a small picnic type shelter at the far end of the compound. Jimmy was introduced to a French priest called Father Marcel. Whitey and the other two men departed, leaving Jimmy Burns with Father Marcel, who gave him instructions in broken English regarding the mass that was about to be celebrated.

Father Marcel explained that he had neither the proper vestments, nor the various accessories that a Catholic priest required to properly celebrate mass. Nevertheless, he thought that God would understand the situation and would

98

recognize his efforts as the best he could do under the circumstances.

Father Marcel had only a small book from which to read the scriptures. It contained a church calendar which enabled Father Marcel to identify the proper feast day to celebrate; however, the complete text of the mass had to be recited from memory. The altar boy duties were somewhat limited, because the huge book containing the Gospels and Epistles was not available to be transported back and forth throughout the mass. Jimmy Burns remembered how he had struggled with the big book as a young boy. There was a small homemade bell to be rung at the proper time, and a couple of small tin cups substituted for the usual cruets, from which wine and water were poured into the chalice.

Promptly at nine o'clock, prisoners from the American compound arrived, accompanied by German guards. French prisoners also gathered within and around the perimeter of the shelter to hear the mass. The German guards who stood outside the shelter seemed to be amused and at the same time wary of the proceedings.

Mass proceeded much as Father Marcel had described it to Jimmy Burns, with substitutions replacing accessories that he lacked. Not having a proper Eucharist, Father Marcel consecrated a large cracker and crumbled it into tiny crumbs, placing a small piece on each tongue of those prisoners receiving Holy Communion. He was not permitted to deliver a sermon, because the Germans believed that religious leaders were capable of sowing discontent among the prisoners. Father Marcel told Jimmy that it took considerable bribing of the guards to even conduct services. It would not have been possible without Whitey's help.

After mass, one of Whitey's assistants arrived and directed Jimmy Burns to follow him back to the entrance of the French compound where Whitey and his other assistant were waiting. The tote bag was now bulging with goods acquired by bartering with French prisoners. Upon arrival in the American compound, Whitey gave Jimmy a pack of cigarettes and a quarter loaf of bread, advising him to keep quiet about it if he would like the job again next Sunday.

That was only yesterday; today he was still standing in line stomping his feet to keep warm. How long had they been standing in this *appell*? It must have been a long time for Jimmy Burns to remember all this. It took several jabs in the arm by Kelsey to bring Jimmy back to reality.

"Pass the word to stand still so the count can be completed." Kelsey said.

Jimmy Burns repeated the instructions to the *kriegie* next to him and stopped stamping his feet.

When the final count had ended, the German sergeant announced that everyone was to return to their rooms, gather their belongings and fall in again in fifteen minutes. The *kommandant* had been ordered to move the Americans from this camp, and since transportation was not available, the entire group would march to a new location.

While gathering up their few possessions, Jimmy and Kelsey learned that the delay in counting had allowed the American commander time to meet with the German *kommandant*. He protested the move and arranged for several sick men to be placed in the nearby hospital. Also, the committee members were busy taking down antenna wire and stowing radios in bedrolls to take along to the next camp.

When the prisoners were once again lined up, it became obvious that the committee people had considerably more gear to transport than the rest of the prisoners. A small wagon was provided to carry the guards' packs, and the committee members were allowed to put their gear on as well. Four prisoners were assigned to pull the wagon.

Daylight was just beginning to show as the column moved out through the front gate to yet another unknown location. The direction of march would determine whether or not chances for escape would improve. Burns and Kelsey talked enthusiastically about future prospects for escape as they trudged along in the snow.

Chapter XI

MARCH AGAIN

The sun was peeking over the horizon as the American prisoners left Stalag 2D and proceeded south toward the main road. They passed the group of civilian prisoners in striped suits that they had seen so many times before. A close look at these poor souls revealed they were very much undernourished.

Their heads seemed too large for the skinny bodies that were hidden under ill-fitting clothing. Blank stares were written on the faces; eyes seemed to bulge from the skull sockets. These prisoners didn't march—they shuffled and stumbled along as best they could. The bodies looked too weak to stand, let alone walk. The feet of many had cloth strips wrapped around them to cover holes in the bottom of shoes. Some may not even have had shoes on their feet. What kind of work could these prisoners possibly perform? wondered Jimmy Burns.

The American prisoners tended to stare at this small group as it passed up the road toward the hospital. As Jimmy Burns focused on one of the men near the end of the column, the man suddenly collapsed and fell sideways into the ditch that bordered that side of the road.

One of the German guards stopped and stood gazing down at the fallen prisoner. A few minutes after the rear of the American column had passed that spot, a shot was heard. Jimmy Burns looked back; the German guard was walking away, moving quickly to catch up to the group of civilian prisoners. Surely those men are all going to die soon, thought Jimmy Burns.

The column of American prisoners quickly reached the main road that ran between Stargard and Stettin. Turning right on this road, they proceeded at a brisk pace in the direction of Stettin. The sounds of battle could be heard to the rear, which was the reason for evacuating the American prisoners from Stalag 2D. Why the Russian, French, and other prisoners were remaining at the camp remained a mystery to the Americans. Perhaps they would be evacuated later.

Instead of feeling cold, Jimmy Burns now felt uncomfortably warm. At each rest stop, Burns and Kelsey found themselves gulping water from their canteens, or eating a handful of snow to quench their thirst. Because only the healthiest prisoners were in this group, the German officer was leading them along at a fast pace. Conversation among the prisoners was almost non-existent, except for comments speculating on where and how far they were going to travel. Somewhere straight ahead, the Allies were winning the war against Germany, as were the Russians to the rear.

The prisoners were bedded down in barns that night in the vicinity of Stettin. There was no food provided that night, only weak coffee. The Germans had not made provision for a meal of any kind, assuming that the prisoners would have stuffed their pockets with every last morsel of food that had been accumulated during the past few weeks at Stalag 2D.

Kelsey and Burns each had a small piece of bread that they had saved from yesterday's ration. They also had a couple of raw potatoes that Kelsey had unearthed in a field during one of the short breaks the group had taken that day.

The two men were so tired they flopped in the hay on the ground floor of the barn without paying any attention to the location they had selected.

Directly above the ground floor was an empty second floor hay mow that required climbing a ladder to reach. Some prisoners climbed up there and found plenty of hay to the rear of the mow. During the night, a tremendous roar went up from prisoners on the ground floor who were being urinated on by someone above them. Most of the prisoners would have to relieve themselves in the night, but would have the decency to go to a corner of the barn where no one was sleeping. The whole night was filled with interruptions as prisoners on the second floor continued to urinate on those below. Burns and Kelsey had to pick up their bedding and move to another spot out of range of these prisoners.

Early the next morning, after a meal of soup-like porridge, the prisoner column headed out again, bypassing the city of Stettin by travelling on back roads. At one stop they saw people working in freshly plowed fields. Some of the workers were American prisoners. Burns and Kelsey walked a short distance out into the field to relieve themselves. By shouting, they were able to engage one of the Americans in a brief conversation. He said his name was Rick Carter and that they were planting potatoes.

"Don't eat these seed potatoes. They're treated with chemicals and will make you sick," Rick advised.

"You look like you're eating pretty good," Kelsey said.

"We get enough to eat. A big meal here at the farm every noon," replied Rick.

"Where do you sleep?" asked Kelsey.

"We stay at a small camp close to the town. The guards bring us out and back every day," said Rick.

"What kind of work do you do?" asked Kelsey.

"Regular farm work, feed animals, clean stalls. Last fall we dug potatoes and harvested grain," was the reply.

"Geez, maybe we should have lied about being non-coms," Kelsey said to Jimmy Burns as they turned away to join the column which was about to move on.

That night there were some sick prisoners as a result of eating seed potatoes. A rumor made the rounds that someone had died because of the chemicals.

Early on the fourth day of this march, the column moved along the outskirts of what appeared to be a fair sized city. This city was quickly identified as Neubrandenburg by Fred King. The results of a recent bombing were in evidence everywhere. Houses and buildings were flattened; railroad tracks were twisted into the air next to large bomb craters that seemed to be everywhere.

After walking around a huge pile of rubble in one of the streets, the prisoner column was halted next to a bombed out building. Broken cartons containing food could be seen inside the building, stacked in a pile like a garbage heap. The guards motioned to the prisoners to help themselves to whatever they could carry. This set off a mad scramble, as the prisoners literally fought with each other over the various bits of food that were to be found in the pile. The Germans called a halt to the battle when it was determined everyone had about all they could reasonably carry.

When Jimmy Burns and Jim Kelsey left the building, their pockets bulged with cans and paper cartons of food. The cans contained either Spam or liver paté; the paper cartons, cheese, crackers, or powdered milk.

Unfortunately, Burns and Kelsey wound up with a lot of powdered milk, which was tasty enough, but further exacerbated the problem of dysentery. Jimmy Burns' ugly blue/gray French overcoat soon had a third color added to the tails of the coat as it dragged in the liquid crap he deposited at every rest stop.

The building had been a warehouse in which American Red Cross parcels were stored. These parcels should have been distributed monthly to prisoners of war. Neither Burns nor Kelsey had ever seen one of the parcels, therefore, they were totally ignorant of what they should be looking for in the pile.

They later learned that American parcels should contain various assortments, including corned beef, Spam, Klim (powdered milk), oleo, salmon, raisins, liver paté, crackers, cheese, sugar, chocolate, an orange concentrate, Nescafe (instant coffee), soap, and cigarettes. Burns and Kelsey had seen many of these items in the possession of British prisoners or committee members back at Stalag 12A and also at Stalag 2D. Whitey, the chaplain's assistant, also seemed to have access to much of the food found in Red Cross parcels. Something was definitely wrong with the distribution system at all stalags.

Evidently, the pile of food in the bombed out warehouse was what was left over after having been previously picked over by German authorities or civilians. The boxes had not burst open due to bombing, but rather had been opened and sorted through before the prisoner column arrived. In talking to other prisoners, Burns and Kelsey learned that no one had found cigarettes, coffee, sugar, chocolate, soap, or the better meat products. Most had found the same items: Klim, liver paté, cheese, and crackers. It was a feast anyway; there was no disappointment. That came later when they learned the full story behind this episode. At least it was food, which the prisoners had seen little of these past few months.

Everyone gorged themselves as the column moved along back roads around the city of Neubrandenburg. First they moved west, then north, finally east to a position well north of the city. The column halted at the entrance to another stalag. This one was known as Stalag 2A.

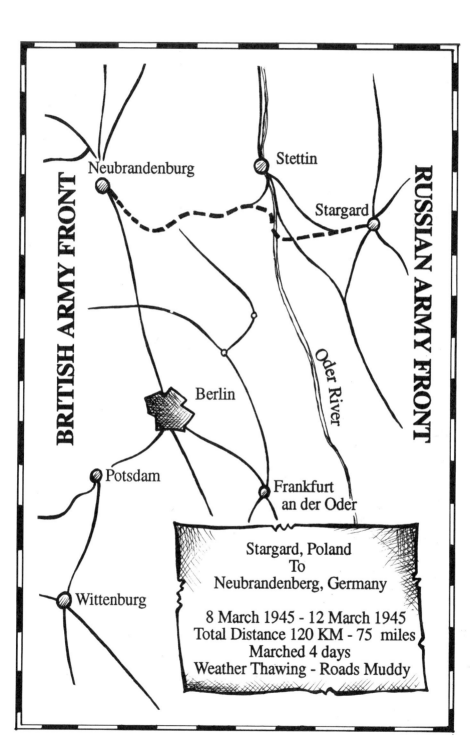

BRITISH ARMY FRONT

RUSSIAN ARMY FRONT

Neubrandenburg

Stettin

Stargard

Oder River

Berlin

Potsdam

Frankfurt
an der Oder

Wittenburg

Stargard, Poland
To
Neubrandenberg, Germany

8 March 1945 - 12 March 1945
Total Distance 120 KM - 75 miles
Marched 4 days
Weather Thawing - Roads Muddy

Chapter XII

STALAG 2A

Unlike the other two stalags the American contingent had been confined in, Stalag 2A showed signs of having been well maintained. The buildings were full, but clean. Previous inhabitants may have been there for a period of time long enough to take pride in their surroundings.

The camp was situated high up on a grassy knoll, surrounded by woods which overlooked a long, narrow valley. A single road provided the only access to the camp from the city of Neubrandenburg.

The Americans, once again, looked like a sorry lot as they entered this stalag. The buildings were already lightly occupied by an assortment of prisoners. These were mostly American Air Force enlisted men, but a few British and French prisoners were in the building assigned to Jimmy Burns and Jim Kelsey. Bunks were stacked three high with bare springs on which to place one's blanket for padding. There were no mattresses available. A stove sat in the end of the room, unused due to a lack of fuel. Coal, straw, and wood shavings had been burned in the stove previously.

Burns and Kelsey chose a triple bunk, the bottom unit of which was already occupied by an American Air Force sergeant named Peter O'Neil. Peter had lived in New York State, not too far from Jimmy Burns' home town.

Alongside, three British prisoners named Jock, Henry,

and Arnold, occupied a triple bunk. Across the aisle, another unit consisted of three French prisoners, named Jacques, Pierre, and Evan. These prisoners had all been in captivity a lot longer than Burns and Kelsey. They all had ample supplies of food stashed away as a result of having received Red Cross parcels at this and other camps.

From these experienced prisoners, Kelsey and Burns learned how to make a *kriegie* forge, a small handmade stove on which one could boil water or reheat soup. It was a rather ingenious device made from cans and tins found in the Red Cross parcels.

A can top was cut with a knife to form radial fins. This fan blade was mounted on a large nail that served as an axle. The fan assembly was mounted inside a milk can through holes punched in the sides. By turning the axle rapidly, wood shavings, once ignited, could be made to flame. The principle was similar to that employed in a blacksmith's forge, thus the name *kriegie forge*. A GI cup filled with water or soup could be heated much faster when placed on top of the milk can.

Peter O'Neil was very helpful to Burns and Kelsey in other ways, sometimes sharing small items such as jam and margarine. He also gave them the butt of his cigarette each time he smoked one.

At Stalag 2A, entertainment was provided by a trio made up of prisoners who were actually members of an Army band when captured. The group consisted of a set of drums, a bass fiddle, and a clarinet. Although the group had been playing together all winter, sheet music for only two songs was available to them: *The Sheik of Araby* and *Red Sails in the Sunset*.

Where the instruments came from was a mystery to Jimmy Burns. The trio played in the hallway of their building with the back door open. Prisoners stood outside listening each time the band played, usually in the evening.

Diaries seemed to be in vogue at Stalag 2A. Many

prisoners exchanged addresses for contact with each other after the war. Others—with food ever present in their minds—noted recipes of various ethnic dishes described to them by other prisoners. It seemed that everyone planned to open a restaurant after returning home.

Jimmy Burns had been carrying a small red notebook in his pocket ever since leaving Stalag 12A. The notebook was actually a primer on German he had obtained for German lessons back in Limburg. Half of the book contained blank pages on which to practice writing German grammar. He had nothing to write with, therefore, traded a few blank pages for a stubby pencil.

Jimmy Burns considered diary writing something that girls did, so abstained from entering very much in his notebook except a log of camp locations and distances traveled.

The British prisoners in the triple bunk next to him constantly sang a love song that intrigued Jimmy Burns. He duly noted the lyrics of this song in his notebook:

"Distance only makes the heart grow fonder.
That is why I long for you.
Far across the sea I ponder,
Wondering, darling, if you're true.
Distance only makes the heart grow fonder,
That is why I long for you."

The French prisoners always countered with their own little song, *Je Attendre*. The song consisted of a few phrases repeated over and over. The translation was roughly, "I wait for you, day and night, I wait for you, every day, your return, I wait for you."

Both the British and French pressed the Americans to sing their favorite love song. The best they could come up with was, *Don't Sit Under the Apple Tree*, which none of them knew completely.

The most important daily event at Stalag 2A was the dividing of a loaf of bread among the specified number of prisoners. Six and seven men to a loaf seemed to be prevalent at Stalag 2A. The German explanation was that bakery supplies were not abundant due to the constant bombing by Allied planes. A wave of excitement would spread throughout the camp whenever the number of prisoners to a loaf was announced as five. Prisoners would greet each other with the German expression, *"Funf mann, ein louf."*

A sharp GI knife always seemed to be available for this task. The prisoners drew lots to determine the order of slicing and choosing among the sliced pieces. The slicer always got last choice, so it was to his advantage to slice equally. The next day the slicer would become first to choose his piece of bread. The order was rotated daily so everyone got to choose in a different position each day.

The slicer would first mark the loaf with fine lines drawn by the knife (five lines for seven slices). The lines would then have to be adjusted, based on the reaction of the group sharing the loaf. There were always complaints; therefore, the procedure took a long time. Slicers tried to cheat by angling the knife downward to produce a thicker slice at the bottom. The penalty for cheating was loss of first pick position the next day. The end pieces or heels were considered to be a good choice because even if thinner, these slices would be heavier.

Once a prisoner selected his piece of bread, it would be guarded carefully. It was held in hand for hours while nibbled at throughout the day. It could not be put down for fear of theft by other prisoners. Neither could it be stowed in pockets for fear of crumbs breaking off. The bread became dirty from sweaty palms, but every last morsel was consumed.

This was not ordinary bread by American standards. It was black in color, containing various grains and molasses. Nutritionally, it was rich and the only means of survival among the prisoners. A loaf of bread weighed one kilo, or approximately two pounds. With seven men to a loaf, each prisoner was receiving about five ounces of nutrition daily.

The soup and coffee provided very little in the way of nourishment. The prisoners estimated that they were losing weight at the rate of between one half to a pound per day.

Another treat at Stalag 2A was a second trip to the showers, along with the usual delousing of clothing. Toilet facilities were better at Stalag 2A, even though they still left a lot to be desired. Warmer weather also made prison life a little more bearable. Rumors persisted that the war would soon end.

The days at Stalag 2A passed quickly for Jimmy Burns and Jim Kelsey. Many days were spent catching up on sleep lost the night before, due to bombing raids on Neubrandenburg. From their bunks, Kelsey and Burns could see the sky light up and hear the roar of exploding bombs. It was like trying to sleep through a thunderstorm.

The stay at Stalag 2A ended abruptly one day, when it was announced that everyone was to line up ready to move to another stalag. There was no delay in counting this time, as rumors persisted that this would be the last move. Supposedly, the Allied forces were closing in from the west, and this move would facilitate liberation from prison camp.

"What if the war ends before we get liberated?" Jimmy Burns said to Jim Kelsey, as they stood in line waiting to move out.

"OK with me," replied Kelsey. "We'll get home that much sooner," he replied.

"Don't you want to get back to the 299th?" asked Jimmy.

"Hell, no, I'm getting out of the Army as soon as I can," replied Kelsey.

"Are you still thinking about staying in after the war?" asked Kelsey.

"Yeah, but I want to get back to the old outfit first. It's important that I continue my career with them," said Jimmy

Burns. He reflected to himself on how improbable this might be and how little control he had of the situation.

The long line of prisoners moved out through the front gate to yet another location.

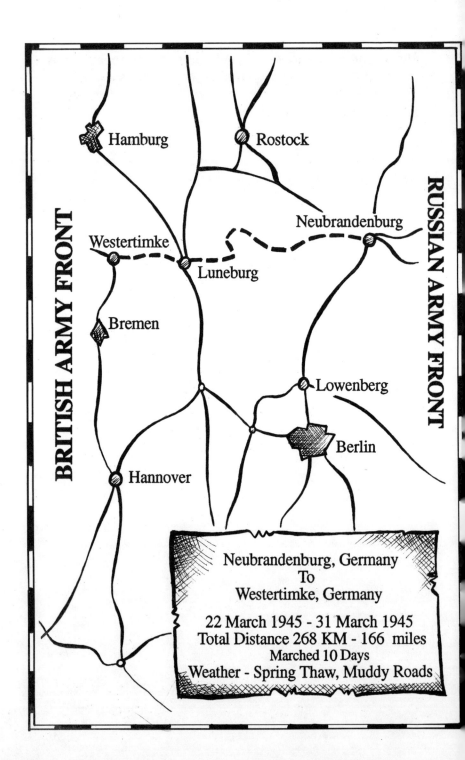

Hamburg

Rostock

Neubrandenburg

BRITISH ARMY FRONT

RUSSIAN ARMY FRONT

Westertimke

Luneburg

Bremen

Lowenberg

Berlin

Hannover

Neubrandenburg, Germany
To
Westertimke, Germany

22 March 1945 - 31 March 1945
Total Distance 268 KM - 166 miles
Marched 10 Days
Weather - Spring Thaw, Muddy Roads

Chapter XIII

LIBERATION

Except for the weather, the trip from Stalag 2A at Neubrandenburg to Marlag/Milag at Westertimke was a routine march. The days were longer, and again, only the healthiest prisoners were included in the group. The sun was getting higher each day, producing slush and mud from the brief spring snow showers. There was very little traffic on the side roads as the prisoner column made its way westward.

The German guards and civilians along the way seemed friendlier. Everyone was convinced the war would soon end, so they wanted to be considered in a favorable light when it finally occurred. Rumors abounded throughout the prisoner column. Every day a new report would make the rounds. The most persistent rumor was to the effect that an advance party had left Stalag 2A one day prior to the main group. Somewhere ahead, this advance party was to meet with the Allies to arrange liberation of the prisoners. This rumor, like all others, proved to be unfounded. The prisoners arrived one evening at a somewhat deserted compound of Marlag/Milag at Westertimke.

It was learned from the guards that this camp was originally designated Marlag/Milag Nord. The camp had been used previously for the internment of naval and merchant seamen, the survivors of ship sinkings on the high seas. The camp had never been completely filled, so it was possible to make available one complete compound to house the American prisoners. The camp was fairly close to the fighting, so liberation seemed a strong possibility.

Westertimke was a small village nearby; Tarmstedt, a larger town in the area; and not too far away was the big city of Bremen. There were other compounds in this camp, but the Americans seemed to be in an isolated section of the camp. A large broad hill extended the entire length of the American compound, hiding all but the rooftops of other buildings in the camp. Eight wooden barracks stood in a row, with a latrine located on the opposite side of a small recreation field. The usual wire fences and guard posts surrounded the compound. Just outside the entrance gate, German guard quarters, a kitchen and the *kommandant's* office sat high up on stilts overlooking the prisoners' barracks. The guards climbed a stairway to gain access to their quarters. This arrangement reminded Jimmy Burns of the scoreboard structures he had seen so often at the American baseball parks.

Living conditions at Marlag/Milag were still quite spartan, but overall it was almost tolerable due to the sudden shift in attitude by the Germans. Roll calls were less frequent and more casual, without jostling or shouting by the guards. The German *kommandant* found Red Cross parcels somewhere and distributed them to the prisoners soon after arrival. With food available at last, the prisoners appeared to be happier and physically stronger.

Of course, there were those prisoners who could never get enough to eat. They resorted to stealing from others at every opportunity. Jimmy Burns and Jim Kelsey worked out a plan to sleep at alternate times, so that one could watch over their meager supply at all times. The plan did not succeed, because Kelsey dozed off one night, allowing a sneak thief named Paul to wipe out their supply of crackers and peanut butter. Kelsey accused Paul of the theft after

116

being tipped off by another prisoner who had been awake guarding his own supply. A fight broke out between the two men with Kelsey coming out the victor. Paul moved out of the barrack and starting sleeping outside, as had many other prisoners. Paul's former partner, a staff sergeant named Jack Dowling, thanked Kelsey for forcing Paul out of the barrack. He had been looking for an opportunity to break away from Paul but felt compelled to look after him, because they had been members of the same infantry platoon when captured.

The next Red Cross parcels distributed were split three ways, so Sergeant Jack shared with Jimmy Burns and Jim Kelsey. One day Jimmy Burns watched as Sergeant Jack sat sketching in his notebook what looked like a map of a battle area.

"What are you drawing?" asked Jimmy Burns.

"I'm trying to sketch the situation my platoon lieutenant sent me into when we were captured." said Sergeant Jack.

He proceeded to explain how his squad had been sent on patrol to check for the presence of enemy in a small village.

"The lieutenant claimed the town was unoccupied, but I could see through the field glasses that plenty of Germans were pouring in from the other side of town. He ordered me to take the patrol in anyway, with a promise that the rest of the platoon would follow if we ran into any trouble."

Sergeant Jack then explained how half way down a slope that overlooked the town, his patrol was pinned down by machine gun fire that seemed to come from a woods on his left.

"Tracer bullets were whizzing overhead. I knew that only Americans could afford the luxury of firing tracers in broad daylight. We couldn't go back up the hill, so we crawled forward right into a German outpost. We figured it was safer in the German bunker, so we surrendered to them. When I looked back, I could see the lieutenant and the rest of the platoon retreating to a road on top of the hill. I called

117

the lieutenant every dirty name I could think of as I sat there with my hands overhead. I'm going to report him as soon as we get out of here."

Similar stories had been related by many infantrymen that Jimmy Burns had discussed capture with.

One of the reasons some of the prisoners moved outdoors was the fear of being killed by either friendly or enemy fire. The battle was coming closer each day. The infantrymen among the prisoners were following a natural instinct to dig holes in the ground for protection. They were very good at determining the type of rounds being fired and the distances at which they were exploding. Allied planes made strafing runs along the road that led to the camp, but always pulled up without firing into the camp. Apparently, they recognized the area as a POW camp. The camp seemed to be directly in line with one hell of a battle that was raging less than five miles away.

One day German soldiers were observed retreating across an open field, directly alongside the camp grounds. Some of the German soldiers fired their weapons in the direction of prisoners who had lined up along the fence to see what was happening. This sent everyone scurrying for protection of the buildings or foxholes.

Soon everyone started digging foxholes in the recreation field or underneath the barracks. The prisoners dug with everything they could find: jackknives, spoons, forks, tin cans, etc. Fortunately, the ground was sandy, therefore, easy to dig in. Still it took a long day and well into the night to dig a hole large enough to hide in. The digging continued the next day as shell bursts started landing in the field adjacent to the camp. Eventually, the recreation field looked like a scene from World War I, with a series of trenches connecting the buildings. One well-travelled trench led directly to the latrine.

Gradually the Allied artillery bursts moved past the camp, in the direction of retreating German troops. Shells from both directions whistled overhead continuously for the next two days. The American prisoners feared that sooner or later German troops would send shells directly into the camp. The Germans had an awesome weapon called a *nebelwefer*. This gun fired rocket-like mortar shells in multiples of a dozen or more. In a manner of speaking, the American prisoners sensed they were living in what could become a graveyard for most of them.

One day the German *kommandant* left on foot with a couple of guards and the camp medical officer. He informed the American commander that he was going to surrender the camp to the Allies as soon as contact could be made. All that day the prisoners huddled in foxholes or trenches, as the noise of battle slowly ebbed. When darkness came, a strange quiet fell on the area, with only the distant rumbling of exploding bombs being heard. Evidently, both sides were in the process of moving their artillery and mortar positions.

Electric power to the camp had been knocked out the previous day. The German guards in the watch towers were without their searchlights, so they shouted back and forth to each other throughout the night. Even without fully understanding the German language, Jimmy Burns could sense a mood of panic among the guards. Sometime before dawn, the German guards deserted all the watch towers and disappeared. They left behind rifles and ammunition, so some of the prisoners climbed the towers to retrieve the weapons.

One of the prisoners in the tower nearest the entrance gate shouted, "Here comes a British tank."

The vehicle turned out to be a small armored reconnaissance car, but it was British and drove right up to the front gate. Cautiously, the hatches of the recon car opened. A sergeant popped his head out and said, "You're liberated, yanks."

The gate was opened, allowing the vehicle to enter the

camp. An American prisoner climbed up to the hatch opening and handed the British sergeant a cup of *kriegie* tea.

The sergeant drank from the cup, thanked everyone, then explained that his was the lead vehicle of a small patrol scouting ahead of the main force. The American prisoners crowded around the vehicle, shaking hands with the rest of the crew as each climbed out to stretch his legs. The sergeant had to plead for quiet while he reported by radio that he had located the POW camp. The poor man had no chance of answering all the questions that were shouted at him.

When asked about the German *kommandant's* party, the sergeant advised that no one believed his story about having the authority to surrender the camp. The British simply "poked him in the ass with a bayonet, and sent him on back with the rest of the Germans captured that day."

Soon a large group of recon vehicles arrived with food, medical supplies, and administrative personnel.

With the liberation of the camp came a certain amount of chaos. Many prisoners wanted to leave the camp. The American commander solved this problem by posting prisoners in the watch towers with orders to shoot anyone attempting to escape. He then took over the German guard quarters with his staff and distributed the remaining Red Cross parcels that were found there.

The British administrative people distributed writing supplies, including forms for every prisoner to fill out. They collected the forms and letters within an hour, dispatching them by special messenger, so that families of the prisoners could be informed as soon as possible.

The excitement of liberation was tempered somewhat for Jimmy Burns, because Jim Kelsey had become sick over the past few days. Kelsey had developed a serious cough, and his throat was so sore he could barely swallow food. For Kelsey to turn down food, he had to be very sick.

The next day several British trucks (or *lorries*, as they called them) arrived at the POW camp. Thereafter, an orderly withdrawal of the prisoners from the camp took place.

The first prisoners to be transported were either sick or needed medical attention for minor wounds. Jim Kelsey left with the first group. It was now the third day of May 1945. Jimmy Burns and Jim Kelsey had been together constantly since the twenty-first day of December 1944. It was with a sad heart that Jimmy Burns waited for his turn to depart.

Chapter XIV

PATH TO FREEDOM

Jimmy Burns was the last prisoner to climb into one of the British trucks that was evacuating prisoners. He was sitting on the last seat on one side of the truck as he had been accustomed to doing every time the squad had traveled by truck prior to capture. This position gave him a full view of the country road the convoy of trucks was traveling as they left the stalag.

The scenery proved to be quite dull. A light rain was falling; the only brightness was a display of white bed sheets draped from the upper windows of German farm houses.

The trucks passed slowly through the streets of Wester-timke, which seemed almost deserted. More bed sheets hung from windows. This was the universal sign of surrender being displayed by German civilians.

Talk among the prisoners was rather subdued. Most were content to sit quietly, probably consumed by their inner thoughts of joy that freedom would soon bring. They were all lacking energy due to the exhilaration and excitement of the past few days.

Jimmy Burns found himself thinking about his Uncle Tip and Sergeant Eddie Boyd once again. Both would have to agree that Jimmy had handled the whole situation as well as could be expected. After all, he was now heading back to the U.S. Army and could continue his duty as soon as he had recovered sufficiently.

He remembered what a kind person his Uncle Tip had been during visits Tip made to the Burns family house years ago. Tip would take all five of the Burns children to the local grocery store and order a five-cent bag of candy for each. Sugar Miller was the store proprietor. He lined up five white bags on the counter, asking each child what candy to put in the bags. This process took at least a half hour, as many changes occurred before the five bags were filled. Later, when the candy was gone, each child found a dollar bill in the bottom of his bag. Uncle Tip had placed the dollar in each bag while the children were selecting their candy.

The convoy of trucks moved on through other small towns, along country roads, finally coming to a halt at a large field dotted with several hundred tents. A sign at the entrance proclaimed it to be a British evacuation camp. The camp was located on the outskirts of Bremen, directly across the road from a military airstrip.

The first order of business for the prisoners was a trip to the latrine, which consisted of the usual military slit trench. Then into a large tent that contained a washstand with hot water, soap and towels available. The prisoners then proceeded to a mess tent for a hot meal of potatoes, stew, rice, curry, tea, bread and butter.

Jimmy Burns was surprised to see that in addition to American prisoners, there were many British colonial soldiers, primarily troops from India. These colonials walked around in British uniforms with small cans tied to their belts. At first Jimmy thought the cans were to urinate in, because the colonials seemed to wander into the woods, rather than use the slit trenches. He finally realized the cans contained water with which to rinse their hands after urinating. What a strange act of cleanliness, Jimmy thought, for people he had always assumed lived in a filthy environment.

The prisoners were given clean blankets and a place to sleep under one of the big tents.

Early the next morning, a breakfast of tea, bread, and jam was served. The American prisoners hung around all morning waiting for the weather to clear so that they could be flown out of this camp.

After lunch, they were marched across the road, where they were loaded into C-47 cargo planes. The C-47 carried cargo or troops with the simple adjustment of lowering bucket seats from their strapped position along the inner wall of the plane. Paratroopers had been transported by this type plane in all airborne missions.

This would be a first airplane ride for Jimmy Burns, as well as most of the others. The ride was bumpy but exciting. Jimmy Burns thought the plane must be over-loaded, as it seemed to take forever to become airborne. The plane appeared to be only a few hundred feet in the air throughout the short ride to Brussels, Belgium. Jimmy Burns could see large bomb craters in the ground as the plane passed over Western Germany, Holland, and finally, Belgium. Later he was advised that the C-47 usually was flown at altitudes of two to three thousand feet.

Many men aboard the plane became airsick and had to heave into the plastic bags provided. Jimmy Burns felt nauseous and had a pounding headache, but managed to keep everything down.

Upon arrival in Brussels, the Americans (no longer called prisoners) were taken by truck to a British facility in the center of town. Here they were housed in a school-like complex formerly used as The Belgium Royal Military Academy.

For dinner, the Americans were treated to a meal of corned beef, potatoes, brussels sprouts, tea, bread and butter, and apricots with cream. At each of the meals so far, portions had been small and seconds were forbidden. There was a danger of overeating and becoming sick.

The men discarded the dirty clothing they had been wearing and were issued brand new British wool uniforms. Clean underwear, socks, even new shoes were available, if required. British boots were hobnailed and stiff, so Jimmy Burns decided to keep his old boots, which were well broken in. The old boots still polished up if enough elbow grease was applied.

The next morning after breakfast, Jimmy spotted Frenchie walking across the courtyard of the complex. They had not seen each other since Westertimke, and the two men had a long conversation concerning the whereabouts of the rest of their group.

They took a walk into the center of Brussels, shopping for souvenirs along the way. The British had even issued everyone military script (about $10 worth).

As they walked along, Jimmy asked Frenchie, "How long have you been here?"

"I got in yesterday about noon," was the reply.

"Have you seen Kelsey?"

"No, but I saw Sergeant Coon leaving here just as I arrived. He said Kelsey was flown to a hospital in France about two days ago."

"Did he say if Kelsey looked OK?"

"He said Kelsey was still having trouble swallowing and couldn't talk. I helped Coon climb into the truck. His feet were killing him. I thought my feet were bad until I saw Coon's the last time."

"They will both be OK. I feel much better after getting cleaned up. Don't you?"

"I almost cried in that shower, it felt so good."

The Grand Place was full of merchants selling flowers, baked goods, and black market foods. It looked as if Brussels was already celebrating the war's end.

Burns and Frenchie splurged for a couple of beers, but had trouble downing them. They passed the beer off to a couple of British soldiers when they realized it was making them sick. The beer was half water anyway, a far cry from the excellent brews they had tasted upon entering Belgium several months ago.

The two men arrived back at The Royal Academy in time for lunch, and shortly thereafter boarded a truck for a ride to Leopold Train Station. They boarded a train that swiftly took them to Namur, Belgium, where they were turned over to the U.S. Army.

Life began anew in typical Army style, by waiting in line for a cup of coffee. It was delicious, being the first real coffee the men had tasted in five months.

Another quick truck ride ended at a U.S. Army facility called RAMP Headquarters. During an interview, Jimmy Burns learned that he was now a Repatriated Allied Military Person (RAMP).

He also learned that he was now Sergeant Jimmy Burns. His promotion mentioned by Captain Stern prior to capture had been approved. A medical examination, including shots, was followed by a delousing shower, after which a new American uniform was issued. After dinner eaten from a new GI mess kit, it was off to bed in comfortable surroundings.

The RAMP facility was located in a military school with dormitories surrounding a courtyard. The clanking sound of mess kits echoed from the walls of the buildings as hundreds of RAMPS traveled to and from the dining room for meals.

The U.S. Army military newspaper, *Stars and Stripes*, issued an *extra*, proclaiming the end of the war in Europe. This news was greeted with great enthusiasm by the RAMPS, although no particular form of celebration took place. Jimmy Burns was surprised by this announcement, because he had not heard one shred of news in the past week. Apparently the excitement of liberation had overshadowed everything else that was going on at the time.

126

Many German POWs were working at the RAMP facility. The American GIs took great pleasure in shouting derisive remarks at them as they passed in the courtyard.

After boarding a train at the Namur station, the group finally left this town at three o'clock in the afternoon. The first few stations passed were familiar to Jimmy Burns: Charleroi, Mabauge, and Aulnoye. He had traveled through these towns earlier, when the 299th had first entered Belgium.

After those few stops, the train proceeded through unfamiliar territory of France until late at night, when it stopped at Le Havre on the English Channel. Another short truck ride brought the group to what looked to be the world's largest tent city, Camp Lucky Strike.

There were several such camps strung along the Normandy coast in the vicinity of Le Havre. Each camp was named after an American cigarette, such as Chesterfield, Camel, Lucky Strike, etc. Each camp held large numbers of American soldiers being processed for return to the USA.

At Lucky Strike, everyone appeared to be a RAMP, but there could have been other soldiers also. The daily routine at Lucky Strike consisted of more interviews, shots, and continuous feeding of light meals.

Eggnog was available to everyone at all times. Large pots of this drink sat in the mess tent ready for the taking throughout the day.

Lectures were conducted relative to conduct expected of a RAMP upon return. It was advised to not be ashamed for having been a POW, but to avoid stressful conversation regarding prison experience.

Warnings regarding over consumption of food and alcohol were injected at every meeting.

Many hours were spent lounging about, playing cards, listening to stories about other POWs' captivity.

This routine was broken one day when two men were reported missing at morning roll call. A massive search located the men's bodies inside a warehouse adjoining the huge mess tent. The men were dead as a result of gorging themselves on food. Empty cartons of fruit, vegetables, meat, potatoes, eggs, syrups, juices, and desserts were strewn about the two bodies when found. The two men had apparently broken into the locked building and feasted throughout the night. Just how anyone could eat so much food was baffling.

Jimmy Burns and Frenchie stayed together most of the time now. They were the only people they had seen from their outfit since leaving Westertimke.

The most entertaining stories of POW life were provided by two happy-go-lucky guys occupying cots near Jimmy Burns and Frenchie. They were an unlikely pair, except that both came from tough neighborhoods in large cities.

One very young man named Tony had grown up in Brooklyn, New York. His much older companion, Ed (nicknamed Whitey due to gray hair), had lived in Chicago. They were both skillful card players (probably cheaters). Whitey admitted that he had worked as a card dealer in Las Vegas in his younger days, but always said that he would not cheat for the small stakes involved.

The last few months of their POW life had been spent in an *arbiet kommando* (work camp) near Berlin. Every day they were taken into the city under guard, issued tools, and spent the day clearing rubble that resulted from bombing raids.

One day Whitey observed two German officers entering the rear of a restaurant by way of an alley that abutted the street they were working on. It happened to be noon time, when the work party was taking its lunch break. Whitey and Tony slipped away from the work party and went into the alley to see what was going on. Through a window they saw the German officers eating lunch at a small table to one side of the chef's work station. When the Germans finished eating, money was left on the table, and they departed through the alley to the main street. Whitey and Tony had ducked into a doorway of a bombed out building near the main street. They were able to hide in the foyer of the building even though the doors had been removed.

For three days they took up position in the bombed out building, observing the same pair of German officers repeating their lunch time habit.

On the fourth day, Whitey and Tony arrived before the two Germans and hid in the doorway. They jumped the Germans from behind, removed their pistols, and robbed them of all their money. The two Germans were both knocked in the head with pistol butts and left in the foyer of the building.

Whitey delighted in repeating this story with loud laughter each time he told it. He said this little robbery was similar to many he had executed as a youngster in Chicago. Actually, it was easier than most because the Germans were old and fat—definitely desk-type soldiers.

Whitey and Tony each produced a German Luger to prove that the story was true. They did not know the value of the German money, but thought it must have been plenty, because it bought them many privileges in the future.

As soon as the work party was moved to another part of Berlin, the two POWs located a restaurant, went to the rear door, and purchased a hot meal of sausage and sauerkraut. The meal was served on regular plates with knives, forks, and napkins. They repeated the process almost every day for a week, even taking their guard along by bribing him. Through the guard they bought cheese, bread, wine, and cigarettes. The money lasted a long time, until they were finally liberated. They still had German marks in their possession when they were telling the story at Camp Lucky Strike. The whole thing sounded preposterous to Jimmy Burns. Still, the German propaganda had always proclaimed that Americans were gangsters.

After two weeks at Camp Lucky Strike, everyone was getting antsy and anxious to go home. When it was announced that another two weeks might elapse before shipping out, Whitey suggested a trip to Paris might be a good way to kill some time. He and Tony amassed even more wealth as a result of their card playing ability.

Jimmy Burns, Frenchie, Whitey, and Tony all walked out of camp to a small crossroads where a sign on the main road showed the direction to Paris. Military vehicles passed by regularly, but after two hours they had not been able to get a ride. Finally, a jeep offered to take two men with them to Paris. Whitey and Tony left in the jeep, shouting the name of a hotel where Jimmy and Frenchie could find them when they, too, got a ride.

Darkness was approaching when Jimmy and Frenchie decided to give up the idea and headed back to Camp Lucky Strike. Good thing they did, because both of their names were posted on the bulletin board for shipment out the next morning. Whitey's and Tony's names were posted also, but they were on the way to Paris and AWOL (absent without leave).

Chapter XV

HOME STRETCH

Almost as soon as Jimmy and Frenchie got aboard the huge boat, they learned it was the USS Monticello, formerly an Italian luxury liner. The ship had been confiscated by the U.S. Navy some time earlier in the war. They were placing their gear on bunks deep in the heart of the ship when a U.S. sailor came along offering pictures of the ship for one dollar each. This transaction took place in secrecy, as it was apparently against Navy rules.

The USS Monticello was typical of luxury liners that cruised the oceans prior to World War II. The U.S. Navy had converted it to a troop ship, but hints of its elegance could still be seen. A large chandelier still hung from the main ballroom which now contained stacks of food supplies and was off limits to all troops. Likewise, a swimming pool and a large dining room had been converted to storage.

Naval guns had been installed on the open decks and anti-aircraft batteries could be seen on the upper levels of the ship. A great source of entertainment during the trip was watching the naval gunners practice fire these weapons.

The ship's crew and Army officers must have occupied staterooms, because the troops being transported were located well below decks in what were formerly open cargo areas. Hammock-type bunks were strung up on steel poles with aisles in between.

Several kitchens must have been added to feed the thousands of soldiers aboard the ship. Food lines stretched out along corridors from the cafeteria-like stations that existed on every deck of the huge ship.

The trip was smooth, since the Monticello was equipped with a modern gyro stabilizing system.

Jimmy Burns received the surprise of his life as he climbed into the upper bunk of a three set hammock system. A paratrooper on the opposite aisle upper bunk said, "Where you from, soldier?"

"Auburn, New York," replied Jimmy Burns.

The paratrooper sat up quickly, shouting, "Christ, so am I!"

With that he extended his hand for a handshake and said, "Joe Shales. I live on Owasco Street. Where do you live?"

"North Street," replied Jimmy Burns, "across from Holy Family Church."

"You didn't go to Auburn High then, did you?"

"No, I didn't."

"That's why I don't know you. I'm one of Father Straub's boys. You know, St. Alphonsos Church."

"I played basketball up there a few times," said Jimmy Burns. "Were you involved with any of Father Straub's teams?"

"The only sport I played was hooky from school." Shales replied.

That conversation set in motion introductions among the six soldiers occupying the two sets of bunks alongside each other. Below Joe Shales were Bob and Fran Hanley, brother paratroopers from Elmira, New York. Frenchie Gregoire was in the bunk below Jimmy Burns. His home town was Niagara Falls, New York. Below Frenchie was Dick Grave who hailed from Rochester, New York.

Joe Shales had been a glider infantryman of the 101st Airborne Division. He had been captured near Maastricht, Holland during an unsuccessful attempt by American and

British paratroopers to secure a bridgehead across the Rhine River in early September 1944. If successful, this would have permitted a quick thrust of ground troops into Germany and made possible an earlier end to the war.

Both Hanleys were members of the 82nd Airborne Division that parachuted into Normandy several hours before the Allied invasion took place on D-Day. Unfortunately, many paratroopers were dropped a long way from the target area that night. Bob and Fran Hanley were captured by the Germans in St. Lo, at least thirty miles distant from the intended drop zone. The two had been together throughout their Army career, and POW camp did not change this.

Dick Grave was with the ill-fated 106th Infantry Division, which took the brunt of the German attack that turned out to be *The Battle of the Bulge.* Jimmy and Frenchie were, of course, both with the 299th Engineers when they were captured in the same battle.

This group of six soldiers hung around together on the ship for the entire voyage. They were reunited later that summer at an R&R facility in Lake Placid, New York. Years later they would each remember those days at Lake Placid with great fondness.

Time passed quickly on the voyage home, with card and crap games going on all over the ship. Walking on the open decks was a great pastime when it was allowed. Otherwise, eating, story telling, and sack time took up most of the day.

Jimmy Burns often reflected on the difference between this trip home and the one he had taken a little over a year ago to get to England. This was seven days of smooth sailing without submarine alerts, lectures, or training—truly a luxury cruise. Space was tight, but showers were available, the ship had a laundry, and the food was edible. In contrast, the trip over had taken two weeks in heavy seas, constant alerts, and dirty, smelly confinement in cramped quarters. Food was rarely consumed on that trip due to seasickness.

Even though time was passing quickly, Jimmy was anxious to call home to tell everyone that he was OK. He thought about the sergeant's stripes he would soon be wearing and wondered what his next assignment might be. Surely he would hold some type of supervisory position, probably training new soldiers. He would certainly try to gain admission to Officer Candidate School as soon as possible.

Even as a sergeant, he would now outrank his Uncle Tip, who had been busted to private. Jimmy had learned this in the last letter received from his mother prior to capture. He didn't understand how this could be possible, until a POW in one of the stalags told him that Fort Levenworth, Kansas contained a large military stockade for soldiers committing serious crimes. Jimmy had always assumed that his Uncle Tip had a routine assignment at Fort Levenworth. Losing his stripes meant that he had done something terrible. Jimmy Burns decided he was no longer going to pattern his career after his Uncle Tip. Maybe he could get an assignment with Eddie Boyd somewhere in the states. Here was a soldier that one could look up to with confidence.

Early on the seventh morning of the trip, it was announced that the Nantucket lighthouse was visible off the starboard side. Everyone rushed topside to get a look at this famous landmark. The same announcement advised the ship would arrive at New York City later in the day.

Activity among the troops below decks picked up in tempo, as everyone scurried about getting names and addresses of new friends and discussed possible meeting places in their home towns. Sure enough—later in the day—the Statue of Liberty appeared, and the Monticello proceeded up the Hudson River to its berth at pier thirty-eight.

That evening many soldiers crowded the dock side open decks of the ship and shouted messages to civilians who

134

were leaning out upper story windows of the pier warehouse. Reporters with notebooks took down names and addresses of soldiers living in the New York area. They promised to phone relatives and to print the names in the daily papers. This noisy, but joyful exchange, lasted about two hours until the troops were advised to return to their quarters. They would not be leaving the ship until the next morning. A train ride to Fort Dix, New Jersey followed the next day for more processing and physical examinations.

It was a sorry looking bunch of bodies that paraded through the physical examination stations at Fort Dix. Jimmy Burns stepped on the scales and watched a good looking nurse adjust the counter weights until they registered one hundred fifteen pounds. Before capture he had weighed one hundred sixty-five, so this represented a loss of fifty pounds. Probably five to ten pounds had already been regained since liberation almost one month ago.

He didn't look too bad compared to some of those around him; still he thought his body looked ugly. A reflection from a glass door at the end of the room showed rib bones protruding like a skeleton's carcass; knobby knee caps stuck out noticeably on skinny legs. Skin drooped from every part of his body; the muscles just were not there anymore. His feet were especially ugly, with black and blue soles, toenails rotting or missing. The toenails still in place were yellow and soft, ready to fall off anytime. As ugly as his feet looked, they did not hurt because there was no feeling in them. His feet were completely numb. A soft cream had been issued to Jimmy Burns for daily application.

One surprise to Jimmy Burns was that he had grown a half inch taller since entering military service. He knew that his weight had steadily increased during the first year, but assumed that he was as tall as he would ever become. Five foot ten and a half and still growing, he thought. Jimmy Burns slowly put his clothing back on and moved in line to the next station, another inoculation. He wondered if the

Army was duplicating some of these shots.

For Jimmy Burns and the others living in New York State, the next move was to Fort Kilmer, New Jersey early the next day. Finally—at this location—Jimmy Burns was able to place a phone call to report that he was on his way home. Because the Burns family did not have a phone, it was necessary to call a very chatty next door neighbor who took forever to call Jimmy's mother to the phone. The woman kept asking all the questions that Jimmy's mother should be asking. There was a long line of soldiers waiting to use the phone, so Jimmy barely had time to tell his mother he was OK and would be home in a few days. Two more days of processing were required before Jimmy Burns boarded a train for the last leg of his trip home.

Part of the processing included an interview regarding what the individual soldier might be requesting as a future assignment after spending sixty days of rest and recuperation. There was still a war on in the Pacific, and no one was going to be let out of the service unless a severe physical handicap existed.

The doctor examining Jimmy's feet had already advised him that he would be able to return to duty after sixty days of rest. The interviewing sergeant said the Army wanted to draw up orders for return to duty as near as was practical to fit the soldier into an assignment that he was best qualified to handle. He doubted that a former POW would be reassigned for duty in the South Pacific. There was no guarantee of this, however. Jimmy advised that he would like to apply for Officer Candidate School in the Engineer Branch at Fort Belvoir, Virginia. The sergeant replied that being a POW would probably prevent such an application from receiving favorable action. He stated that Jimmy's service record would show this POW period as a black mark just like other offenses, such as AWOL and desertion. He further indicated that this episode would rule out promotions for Jimmy Burns even if he stayed in the service as an enlisted man. Jimmy was shocked by this statement, but still accepted the sergeant's word as gospel. With this revelation, Jimmy thought his next assignment might well be discharge from the service as soon as he completed the R&R.

The sergeant agreed to draw up orders sending Jimmy to Fort Belvoir for further assignment as an enlisted man. Headquarters for the Engineering Branch of the Army were located at Fort Belvoir. There were plenty of other opportunities there, and Jimmy definitely wanted to stay in this branch of the service. Sixty days sounded like a long time before he would have to make up his mind about whether or not to pursue an Army career.

The following day found Jimmy Burns on a train that took him to New York City where he was to catch another train for upstate New York. None of his friends were with him now. Even Joe Shales from his home town had become separated due to alphabetical processing, which the Army always adhered to. The train was completely filled with soldiers, all heading into New York for transfer to other trains which would take them home.

The soldier sitting next to Jimmy Burns was dark complexioned and spoke with a Spanish accent, which could also be classified as broken English. He asked Jimmy to look at his orders, because something didn't read just right to him. He admitted that he could not read all of it clearly, but thought he should be heading for Miami instead of New York, because he was a citizen of Cuba.

His orders stated that he was to transfer in New York to a DL&W train, which would take him to Olean, New York. From there he was to find a bus or taxicab to Cuba, New York.

Jimmy Burns had never heard of Cuba, New York, but by inquiring up and down the aisle of the car he found someone from Buffalo, New York, who confirmed that Cuba was a small village near Olean.

When the train arrived in New York City, Jimmy took the soldier to the Military Transportation Office located in the terminal. Surely, they could work out the problem. This was a typical Army foul-up by a clerk who may not have known there was such a country as Cuba. What a mess it would have been, if the poor soldier had not sought out help.

Jimmy Burns wandered about New York City for several hours before boarding a train for Syracuse, New York late that night. All this time he had to lug a big barracks bag that contained all his clothing and personal items.

From Syracuse he would have to take a bus to his home town of Auburn, New York. New York City held plenty of wonderment and awe for a small town boy, but Jimmy was nervous in the big city, and therefore confined his sightseeing to within a few blocks of the train station. Grand Central Station was big enough to get lost in all by itself.

Jimmy Burns had barely settled into his seat on the train to Syracuse when he spotted a soldier named Bob Shaw that he had known in high school several years ago. Bob Shaw was very drunk, and could not seem to focus long enough to recognize Jimmy Burns. Bob was a few years older and had been a member of the National Guard when it was activated in 1940. He rambled on about the terrible war he had left in the South Pacific and boasted of his wounds received on December 7, 1941 at Pearl Harbor.

Jimmy Burns gave up trying to identify himself to Bob Shaw and walked back to his original seat in the coach. He did not want to discuss war with anyone, let alone a drunken soldier from his home town.

He tried to sleep, but the clickety-clack of the train wheels on the track kept him awake. He worried about how he was going to explain to other soldiers like Bob Shaw that he had been a prisoner of war. Now he was hoping that the R&R orders would arrive soon, so that his stay at home would be a short one.

At some point he must have dozed off, because he was

awakened by an announcement that the next stop was
Syracuse, New York.

Chapter XVI

JOYFUL REUNION

Jimmy Burns walked the two blocks from the bus station to his home, still carrying the big duffle bag that contained his gear. His heart started to pound as he walked up North Street, past the Episcopal church with its big steeple that was something of a landmark.

Several apartment houses later, he was standing in the doorway of apartment #3, 76 North Street. It was almost seven thirty in the morning when he opened the front door, which was never locked.

He stepped in and shouted, "Hi, Mom, I'm home."

Jimmy Burns knew it was Monday, because his mother was doing laundry in the kitchen. The old Maytag was swishing away, making such a racket that his mother did not hear him. Nothing has changed, thought Jimmy. Mother would do laundry on Monday during an earthquake, tornado, hurricane, or any other national disaster.

His mother must have sensed that someone had entered. She peeked around the corner through the door opening, leaped over a pile of clothes, and shouted, "Oh my God, Jimmy is home."

She met him in the foyer doorway and burst into tears.

Upstairs the bathroom door opened, and a voice said, "Did you call me, Marg?"

Jimmy's mother blubbered, "Bill, Bill, come down.

Jimmy is here."

Jimmy's dad came bounding down the stairs with half his face still lathered in shaving cream. The three of them stood there in a triple hug for several minutes crying tears of joy.

Next, his sister Ann came down—still wrapped in a robe. She had just finished the night shift at the local hospital as a nurse and was still in the process of undressing to go to bed.

Being very professional, Ann said, "Welcome home."

Marylou showed up next all dressed up to go to work. She had graduated from high school within the year and was interested in two things: clothing and boys.

Her first remarks were, "Wait until the girls in town see you in that uniform. I have been telling them how handsome my brother was."

Even though Jimmy knew he was skinny looking in his poor-fitting uniform, it was just like Marylou to have nothing but praise for her older brother.

Little Stella was still in her nightgown when she came down the stairs. As an eighth grader, she should have been all dressed for school by now. She hardly knew her brother Jimmy, he had been away so long. Stella said, "Oh, boy, now you can attend my eighth grade graduation."

That accounted for everyone except brother Mike, who was still sleeping. If there was anything Mike could do better than anyone else, it was sleep. Stella's job every morning was to wake up Mike when she left for school. Mike could jump out of bed, wash, dress, eat breakfast, and run the two hundred yards to school in a little less than fifteen minutes. He had done this for years, seldom being late for school.

Jimmy's mother made a few futile attempts to wake Mike by calling to him from the bottom of the stairway. She was about to go upstairs when Jimmy stopped her, advising that he would wake him later.

He reached into his duffle bag and took out a little

souvenir gift for each member of the family.

Jimmy took the little souvenir he had brought for Mike and went upstairs to awaken him. When he saw Mike lying there in bed, he realized how much his brother had grown since seeing him last.

Jimmy touched Mike on the shoulder and said, "Wake up, Mike, it's Jimmy."

Mike rolled over, mumbled, "Hi, Jim," and fell back to sleep.

Jimmy Burns looked at the big kid in that little bed and wondered how he was ever going to share that bed with him again. They had always slept together in the past.

Jimmy put Mike's gift on the dresser and returned downstairs to rejoin the rest of the family. Everyone took turns filling him in on important events that happened to them while he was away. Most of it he had learned from letters written by his mother but he listened any-way—always changing the subject whenever he was asked to talk about his POW experience.

Jimmy's mother showed him telegrams they had received from the War Department and related a story about a novena she had made just prior to receiving the telegram advising that he was alive.

It was almost noon when Jimmy Burns decided that he needed some sleep. He had been enroute from Fort Dix for more than twenty-four hours with little sleep on the train or bus. He slowly climbed the stairs, turned into the front bedroom, and looked sleepily at his father's big bed with the fresh linen his mother had put on it.

He was taking off his clothes when he was startled by the ringing of a doorbell. He looked out the window in time to see the mailman descending the front steps. As was his custom, the mailman had run the bell and shouted, "Mail-man."

For just an instant Jimmy Burns thought he had heard someone say, *"Funf mann."*